'I have an idea,' he said abruptly. 'A solution.'

She stiffened. It entered her mind that he was quite deliberately using his considerable sexual magnetism to persuade her into something she might regret. With an effort she took a step away, in an attempt to escape that seductive aura.

He reached for her, his hands closing about her upper arms. 'Listen.' He paused, and for a moment she thought doubt, uncertainty, entered his eyes. Then he said, 'There's one way out of this dilemma, if you agree.'

Warily, she stared at him. She mustn't be influenced by the effect he had on her, the physical responses that clamoured to be set free from the stern restraint she kept on them. 'Agree to what?'

He was looking at her as though willing her to something, his gaze hypnotic. His jaw jutted, and she saw the muscles of his throat move as he swallowed. He said, 'To marry me.'

Daphne Clair lives in subtropical New Zealand, with her Dutch-born husband. They have five children. At eight years old she embarked on her first novel, about taming a tiger. This epic never reached a publisher, but metamorphosed male tigers still prowl the pages of her romances, of which she has written over thirty for Harlequin Mills & Boon, and over fifty all told. Her other writing includes non-fiction, poetry and short stories, and she has won literary prizes in New Zealand and America. Readers are invited to visit Daphne Clair's website at www.daphneclair.com

Recent titles by the same author:

THE DETERMINED VIRGIN
CLAIMING HIS BRIDE
THE MARRIAGE DEBT
THE RICCIONI PREGNANCY

THE
BRUNELLESCI
BABY

BY
DAPHNE CLAIR

MILLS & BOON®

First published in Great Britain 2004
Paperback edition 2005
Harlequin Mills & Boon Limited,
Eton House, 18-24 Paradise Road, Richmond, Surrey TW9 1SR

© Daphne Clair 2004

ISBN 0 263 84117 0

Set in Times Roman 10½ on 12 pt.
01-0105-47571

Printed and bound in Spain
by Litografia Rosés, S.A., Barcelona

CHAPTER ONE

THE passport control officer quickly scrutinised the dark-haired, green-eyed young woman waiting at the other side of the desk.

She tensed, trying not to show apprehension as he returned his gaze to the photograph in the passport he held. Finally he said, 'Liar.'

Her heart accelerated its beat and her cheeks flushed.

He looked up again. 'Liar Cameron?'

Nearly fainting with relief, she said, 'No, it's *Lee-ah*.' And more firmly, 'My name is *Lia* Cameron.'

'Sorry—Lia.' He flipped over the page. 'You've been to Australia before?'

'Yes.'

The man stamped the page before handing back the passport with a grin. 'You kiwis just can't stay away, eh? Enjoy your holiday.'

Her knees shook as she proceeded to the arrivals hall and found the baggage carousel for the Auckland to Sydney flight. It wasn't the first time 'Lia' had been mispronounced. A guilty conscience was responsible for her almost making a fool of herself back there.

When her suitcase appeared she lifted it off the carousel and flipped the label to check. *Lia Cameron.* 'That's me,' she muttered aloud.

She took a bus to the Sunshine Coast, found a hotel and paid cash in advance for her room, not wanting to use her credit card.

Tomorrow she would hire a car and find the Brunellesci mansion. And Zandro Brunellesci.

Ice snaked down her spine. Alessandro Gabriele Brunellesci was a formidable foe, accustomed to crushing anything—or anyone—who got in his way. Including Lia.

Anger sharpened by grief dispelled the cold fear. Stress and tragedy had given her a strength she hadn't known she possessed. Zandro would discover she couldn't be crushed, bullied, and he wouldn't find it so easy to get rid of her. Too much was at stake—a child's whole life. The righting of a terrible wrong.

She couldn't return to New Zealand until she'd done what she'd come here to do. And she would not go home alone.

The Brunellesci home was guarded by wrought-iron gates set in a high brick wall. Tall gum trees and silver birches screened the house, allowing through the iron bars only glimpses of mellow golden stone and big windows. There seemed to be a garage underneath that lifted the first floor enough to give the rooms a view over the wall to the sea, and a third level shaded a wide balcony.

After driving slowly past she parked a little farther along the broad street, in the shade of a tree overhanging the wall of another expensive-looking home. Across the road an expanse of dark, coarse grass was broken by more trees, and an awning sheltered a children's play area from the Queensland sun that was still wintry-mild, as yet not holding the full force of the coming summer. Beyond the swings and slides and a jungle gym, a swathe of silvery sand was licked by milk-white tongues of foam edging the blue-green ocean.

Cars intermittently left the street or cruised into it. A young woman holding the hands of two small girls sporting identical blond ponytails emerged from one of the houses and crossed to the park.

Twins? But leaning forward with naturally quickened interest to peer through the windscreen, she saw that one was a little bigger than the other; perhaps a year or so separated them.

A sleek black saloon with tinted windows slid from between the imposing gateposts of the Brunellesci house. Impossible to see inside the car, or even guess if it held only the driver or had passengers.

People strolled down to the beach as the sun moved higher up the pale sky, but not many walked along the street.

This wasn't getting her anywhere. She rummaged in her bag, donned wraparound sunglasses, then twisted her hair and piled it inside a wide-brimmed natural-straw hat that she pulled low over her forehead, and took a brand-new paperback book from the glove box.

There were wooden seats near the play area, back-to-back sets. She chose one facing the road and the wrought-iron gates of the Brunellesci house, pretending to read while watching the gates. The seat escaped the shade cast by the awning, and the morning sun gently warmed her shoulders, bared by the sleeveless cream shirt she wore with cotton shorts.

Still no sign of movement from the house. Then after some time a woman with a child in a pushchair emerged, accompanied by a tall, white-haired man walking with the help of a stick.

The gates slid open to let them through, and they

paused at the edge of the pavement before crossing to the park and the play area, passing the young woman apparently absorbed in her reading.

They hadn't even noticed her. Lowering the book to her lap with shaking hands, she took a deep breath, willing herself not to turn, not to give herself away. She could hear the woman's voice, rising and falling in the exaggerated way people spoke to babies, and a brief, deep male rumble from the man, over a stream of happy babble from the child.

Her heart contracted. Feigning nonchalance, she stood up, closing the book, and without looking directly at them skirted the group and settled herself on the grass under a tree, her back against the trunk.

The old man leaned on his stick, watching while the woman pushed the child on a baby swing, not too high.

Small, round face shaded by a blue hat, chubby legs emerging from blue cotton overalls, clearly the little boy was enjoying himself. The sound of his delighted laughter carried on the clear air.

He's being well cared for.

Maybe she should abandon her mission, leave. But the cowardly thought was quickly dismissed. One glimpse didn't tell the whole story.

She turned her attention to the woman, probably in her mid-thirties, with a pleasantly attractive face framed by short brown curls, and a curvy but fit-looking body, the waist accentuated by a white belt about a plain green dress worn with white flat-heeled sandals. A nanny. Someone they'd hired to take charge of the baby.

When the child was lifted from the swing and the group went down to the beach she made herself stay where she was, then after a while get up and go back to the car, where she watched until they returned to the house and disappeared inside the gates.

After some time had passed with no further activity discernible she started the car, drove slowly by once more, then accelerated and turned a corner, taking a route that passed the rear of the mansion.

There were other homes backing onto it, but she glimpsed behind them the same high brick wall. Any thought of secretly making her way into the house was unfeasible. Not that she'd seriously considered that, knowing it was burglar-alarmed to the teeth.

At least now she knew where the baby was, that he hadn't been sent off to some secret hideaway or remote country estate to be raised in isolation.

Time to consider her strategy.

The next morning she parked in the same place and waited. Again the trio of woman, elderly man and baby appeared. The woman carefully looked right and left and right. Her gaze seemed to linger on the parked car, and she turned to say something to the white-haired man before stepping onto the road with the pushchair.

Imagination, surely. But caution warned, *Don't be conspicuous. Stay in the car, out of sight.*

The child was enjoying his swing. When the woman lifted him out he pointed to a low slide, and she took him to it and supported him as he swooped to the ground, then repeated the process. Each time he reached the bottom he clapped his hands together in gleeful approval.

His grandfather took a seat under the shade of the awning and placed the walking stick between his knees, a slight smile on his thin lips. For a man who had built an empire from nothing after entering Australia as a penniless Italian immigrant fifty-odd years ago, earning a reputation for drive and hard-nosed business practice equalled only by the son to whom he had passed the reins, he looked almost benign.

Tough, strong men, according to medical studies, grew mild in old age with the gradual loss of testosterone.

His son Zandro was in his early thirties, with a long way to go before that happened. Maybe old Domenico would be an easier target. And he must surely still have some influence with his son.

Intent on the group in the park, she hadn't seen the big black car approach—so silently she didn't hear it either until it swerved across the road and stopped in front of hers, nose to nose.

Immediately a man flung open the driver's door and leapt out. Her heart plunged even before he'd covered the few strides to her side and hauled open the door. Her hand went to the ignition key in an automatic but futile attempt at escape.

Long, hard fingers closed about her wrist. She was jerked from her seat with no time to put up more than the feeblest resistance, and backed against the rear door, her assailant's broad shoulders blocking her view.

The hand that wasn't holding her wrist in an iron grip slammed down on the roof of the car, trapping her while fiery, obsidian eyes in a spare, strong face seared her with an expression at first suspicious, then disbelieving.

'*Lia?*' His voice was tempered steel in a velvet sheath.

She swallowed, in danger of melting under the gaze that now held a heat like banked coals. There was no mistaking who he was. 'Zandro,' she said.

Unlike the father he strikingly resembled, the younger Brunellesci showed no hint of benignity. Suffocatingly aware of his size, his physical power, the furious incredulity in his eyes, and her veins throbbing in the wrist encircled by his bone-breaking hold, she tried to gather courage to stand up to him.

Black brows snapped together. 'What the hell are you playing at?'

Don't crack. He's only a man. 'I'm not *playing* at anything.' She thrust her chin forward. 'Let go my wrist.'

Zandro Brunellesci blinked, thick dark lashes momentarily blanking out the fiery stare, and when they lifted, a faint surprise lit his eyes.

Lia had never directly challenged his authority, his right to do as he liked with her or any member of his family.

But this was another Lia, one who wouldn't be pushed around, who knew what she wanted and had come to get it. Who'd refuse to take no for an answer, regardless of what it cost her—or him.

For a second longer he stared down at her, not moving, before abruptly releasing his hold, but his other hand didn't leave the car roof and he still loomed over her.

Automatically she cradled her aching wrist with her free hand, then dropped them both to her sides, not wanting to show him any weakness.

To her surprise he reached down and took her hand, more gently this time, though firmly overriding her resistance.

He frowned down at the reddened skin, and she saw his mouth tauten, a sudden whiteness appear at one corner. 'I didn't mean to hurt you,' he said, his voice altering to a low rasp. 'I got a shock.'

'You gave me one too,' she said tartly. 'Not to mention a bruise, probably.'

His remarkable eyes flashed as he let go her hand. A hint of puzzlement flickered across his face when she stared defiantly back at him. Again there was a change in the dark depths, a spark of something that caught her unawares and made her breath quicken.

Impatiently he shook his head, and shifted, bending to remove her car key from the ignition. He closed the door and, ignoring her protest, locked it, shoving the key into his pocket. 'You'd better come to the house and get some ice on that.' Once more he glanced at her wrist, then he laid a careful but compelling hand on her arm, just above the elbow.

Her instinct was to draw away, condemn his high-handedness and demand her key before driving off. But although it could hardly be called an invitation he was suggesting an entrée to the house, and expediency dictated she shouldn't turn the offer down.

This confrontation had been inevitable sooner or later, and so what if she didn't feel prepared for it right now? The fact was she never would be. She'd been procrastinating under the excuse of scouting the enemy territory and refining her plan. Now an unexpected opportunity had arrived she should grasp it with both hands.

Zandro's fingers at her elbow seemed to emanate tongues of fire and her nerves were jumping. Strange sensations that she'd never felt before, but then she'd never before been in this situation. Normally a scrupulously honest person, she was about to embark on a reluctant deceit that it would take all her resolution and strength of mind to carry out.

It's not too late, whispered a craven inner voice. She could still back out. Insist on leaving, take the first flight straight back to New Zealand.

She looked up at Zandro Brunellesci's face, a face set like granite in an expression of controlled ferocity. Her heart quailed, and the words she'd been about to utter dried on her tongue. The man was frightening in his very restraint. But she'd faithfully, solemnly promised to go through with this. If she didn't live up to that promise she would never forgive herself.

He locked his own car and she allowed him to guide her along the pavement. At the entrance to the drive a numbered keypad and a discreet microphone with a sign saying Press For Entry were fixed to one of the brick posts. But Zandro slid a hand into a breast pocket of the impeccable suit he wore and must have touched some remote-control gadget. The gates silently parted and he ushered her inside.

When the gates clicked shut behind them she shivered visibly, irrationally feeling that she was being locked into some kind of sinister prison.

'Are you all right?' Zandro paused under one of the trees, the softly twisting leaves overhead making moving patterns of sunlight that gleamed on his sleek, almost black hair. The question sounded grudging, reluctant.

'Yes. It's just coming from the sun into the shade.'

The broad tree-lined drive wasn't very long and soon they were mounting stone steps beneath a cool overhang supported by substantial pillars.

Zandro punched numbers into another keypad by the heavy door and swung it open, then steered her across a tiled floor to a large, airy room furnished with dark-wood occasional tables and cabinets, and tapestry-fabric chairs. 'Sit down, Lia,' he said, halting at a deep, velvet-covered antique sofa. 'I'll get some ice.'

She wondered why he didn't just summon a servant. Perhaps he didn't want them asking how she'd been hurt; it could be embarrassing for him.

He was back quite quickly, carrying a bowl of crushed ice and a hand-towel which he fashioned into a cold compress. Then he knelt on the floor before her to wrap the cloth firmly about her wrist, tucking the end in to hold it.

'You're good at this,' she said involuntarily, unable to hide her surprise.

'I've dealt with sports injuries.' He was on a level with her now, and only inches away as he looked up from his task, his gaze somehow distant despite his physical proximity.

She could see a few fine lines at the corners of his eyes, and the faint beard-shadow on his taut, closely shaved cheeks. A hint of some pleasant, woodsy scent came from him—aftershave or something like it. His hair was glossy black, with a slight wave. He'd removed his tie and opened the collar of his white shirt, revealing naturally olive skin. She found herself fascinated by the almost invisible beat of a pulse at the base of his throat.

Dragging her attention from it, she said, 'You still play?' Vaguely she recalled some mention of him having been a tennis champion in his earlier years.

'Enough to keep me fit. Rest your arm here.'

He placed it on the arm of the sofa, but she immediately lifted it away to support it with her other hand. 'I'll make the upholstery wet.'

Zandro looked briefly nonplussed. With the kind of money his family had, she supposed a spoiled sofa would be a minor inconvenience. But he said, 'I'll fetch another towel.'

He brought a larger one and folded it so there was little chance of water seeping through. When he straightened from arranging it for her he stood regarding her with a penetrating stare before swinging away to sit in a chair facing her.

'What are you doing here, Lia?'

She hesitated, moistening her lips. This was the point of no return. Her last chance to retreat, walk away. Steadying her voice with an act of will, she said, 'I've come for my baby. To take him home.'

Zandro was so still, so expressionless, he might not have heard her. Seconds passed, and then an almost infinitesimal movement showed in his cheek, a slight tightening of the muscles in his jaw. 'I don't think so,' he said.

Raising her chin a fraction, she fixed her gaze unwaveringly on his darkling one. 'He belongs with... with me.'

Something glimmered in his shadowed, hostile eyes. 'You think I'll give him up to you, just like that?'

'I'm his mother!' Putting every ounce of conviction she could into her voice.

'And I'm his legal guardian, committed to looking after his interests.'

The words sounded more suited to a business meeting than a discussion of a child's needs. 'You mean the interests of the Brunellesci dynasty.'

The resolute brows rose a scant millimetre. 'I hardly think the family business qualifies as a dynasty.'

'Isn't Pantheon listed as one of the top ten richest

Australian companies, worth how many millions? Or is it billions?'

His gaze sharpened. 'Is that what this is about?' The steel in his voice was unsheathed. 'It isn't your son you've come for, is it? Let's dispense with the pretence, shall we?'

Her eyes widened, and her stomach made a sickening revolution. 'How—' she started to say weakly.

But he wasn't listening. 'You're hoping we'll pay you to go away again and leave him with us.'

The accusation stunned her at first. Then she shot to her feet. 'That's a *foul* suggestion! You're even worse than I thought!'

He too stood up, meeting her hot-eyed gaze with a glittery stare. 'I might return the compliment.' A small pause, and then, 'If I'm wrong, what *do* you really want?'

'I told you! I want Dominic—I want…my son.'

'You gave him up.'

A brutal reminder, further hardening her against him, if that were possible. 'I wasn't myself, didn't know what I was doing.'

'And,' he inquired with deadly irony, 'are you *yourself* now, Lia?'

Stupidly, the question sent her heart into a crazy, terrified revolution. She knew her face showed confusion, perhaps guilt, and he gave a short, humourless laugh. 'Were you thinking of kidnapping Nicky? You'd never have got away with it.'

Nicky? Who…? After a moment light dawned. Dominic had acquired a nickname. 'I wasn't going to kidnap him!' No need to tell him the idea had been briefly considered, and discarded.

'So why lurk about watching the house?'

'What makes you think I was?' *Neither confirm nor deny.* That was safest.

He looked impatient. 'My father and the nanny saw you yesterday, and she recognised the same car parked in the same place today. They thought your behaviour was suspicious, and called me.'

On a cell phone, she presumed. They hadn't yet returned from the beach. 'I wanted to be sure Dominic was still here. And being properly cared for.'

'He's had the best care possible,' Zandro said.

'The best that *money* can buy, you mean.' Allowing her scepticism to show. 'You hired a nanny.'

His head tilted slightly. 'My mother is no longer able to keep up with a lively young child. And I have a business to run. Barbara is highly qualified and came from a very reputable agency. She's extremely competent.'

'A professional can't afford to get too emotionally involved with her charges.'

'A good nanny is better for a child than an incompetent mother.'

'Incompetent?' Her voice shook with anger.

He was looking austere again. 'You know you were incapable of looking after a child, Lia.'

'A temporary state!' she argued. 'That you took advantage of to snatch Dominic away!'

'We took responsibility for a vulnerable member of our family. His safety and wellbeing was our first priority. He's a Brunellesci, after all.'

'He's a Cameron!'

'The fact that his father didn't marry you is immaterial,' Zandro said. 'Rico's name is on the birth certificate, and my parents have accepted Nicky as their grandchild.'

'That doesn't make him yours—or theirs.' If the Brunellescis had charge of his upbringing, would they turn that laughing, innocent little boy into an unfeeling, hard-headed brute in a business suit, like his uncle and his grandfather? It didn't bear thinking of. 'A mother's claim comes first.' Rashly she added, 'Any court would back that!'

'The court would take into account the best interests of the child. A mother with a drug dependency who abandoned her baby isn't a very trustworthy prospect.'

'I don't…' She should probably have expected this, but she could feel herself shaking, and clenched her hands to hide it. 'He wasn't abandoned, and you're wrong. I *don't* have a drug dependency.'

'You're clean?' He cast her a razor-edged look. 'You look better,' he conceded. 'But how long can you stay away from the stuff?'

Her teeth snapped together. 'I was never an addict. My mind was…was mixed up.'

'That's an understatement,' he said dryly. 'You hardly knew what day it was, and as for looking after a newborn baby—if I hadn't stepped in Nicky would have been sent to a child welfare home.'

'I was in shock! Grieving for your brother, my… my—'

'Your lover,' Zandro supplied.

'The father of my child! The child you took away.'

After that, to Lia nothing had seemed to matter any more. She'd taken pills to ease the pain, to help her sleep, to blot out the world and its cruelty. Until time and emotion blurred and she was living in another dimension, a blessedly vague world where she felt nothing, remembered nothing, knew nothing except that she had to have more pills, and more…

'I tried to help you,' Zandro said.

A renewed flare of anger rose. She must stay calm, keep her wits about her. 'I don't recall that you ever offered *help*,' she said flatly.

He looked exasperated, then almost weary. 'I don't suppose you recall much at all, zonked out of your skull as you were.'

A faint unease stirred deep down. Had things happened at that time that she didn't know about?

Sounds at the front door interrupted them. It opened and there were voices in the hall.

Instinctively she turned her head, catching a glimpse of the nanny crossing the hallway, the baby in her arms.

Without thought she took a step towards them, but Zandro's hand closed about her arm, and she halted, then pulled away from him.

The old man appeared, blocking her view, and came to a stop in the doorway of the room, leaning on his cane.

At the sight of her he straightened, and his expression turned icy. Shifting his gaze to Zandro, he said, his accent betraying his Italian origin, 'What is that woman doing here?'

It felt like a slap in the face. Renewed antipathy surfaced as she squared her shoulders and confronted him. 'I have a name, Mr. Brunellesci,' she said. *'Lia.'* She pronounced it like a challenge. 'And a right to my son.'

'You have *no* rights!' He thumped his cane on the tiled floor. Stepping into the room, he waved the walking stick at her before using it to steady himself, his knuckles whitening. 'How can you dare to come here again?'

'Papa,' Zandro interrupted, his voice quiet but authoritative, 'don't upset yourself. I'll deal with this.'

The old man's glare swivelled to his son. If Domenico had mellowed in old age it certainly wasn't apparent now. Finally he nodded, perhaps satisfied that Zandro was as relentless as himself, and with a parting haughty scowl at the intruder and a muttered word that sounded like *'Cagna!'* he turned and left the room, the muffled tapping of his stick gradually fading.

Zandro said, 'Please sit, Lia.'

After a slight hesitation she did so, back straight, not sinking into the tempting softness. 'What did he call me?'

Zandro remained standing. A movement of his hand dismissed her question. 'It's not important. How's your wrist?'

Numbed. 'I'm sure it will be all right.' But she would retain the compress a little longer. He'd find it harder to throw her out while she still had it on. 'Your father hates me.'

'He loves Nicky.'

As if it followed logically. 'Is it love?' she queried. 'Or possessiveness?' Dominic, named after his grandfather at Rico's wish, was the senior Brunellesci's only grandchild, the sole member of the new generation. 'You're not married yet, are you?' she asked Zandro. 'If you have children, what happens to Dominic?'

He frowned. 'He will still be Rico's son, a Brunellesci. Nothing can change that.'

'He's my son, too. Nothing can change *that*.'

A flicker of acknowledgement momentarily lessened the chilly hostility in his eyes. Then his mouth hardened and the pitiless expression returned. 'You relinquished your rights.'

'You bullied me into signing those papers when I couldn't stand up to you!'

'Bullied?' Reciprocal anger lit his eyes. 'Bribery I'll admit to, but bullying? I had no need to resort to that. You were only too happy to take the money and run.'

The accusation took her breath. She opened her mouth to deny it, then reminded herself to think before she spoke. Almost choking on the words, she said, 'It had nothing to do with money! At the time it seemed the best thing for him. But there are more important things for a child than money and what it can buy.'

'Agreed,' Zandro said. 'A family, for one thing.'

'*I'm* his family!'

His mouth turned down in a sceptical sneer. 'Forgive me if I find this sudden maternal concern difficult to believe.'

'It's not *sudden* at all! You don't know how hard it was, how much heartbreak…' She stopped there, her eyes stinging, and quickly turned her head, trying to stem the threatening tears, her teeth sinking savagely into her lower lip. Weeping in front of this unfeeling man was humiliating.

One tear escaped and unthinkingly she lifted her towel-encased arm to swipe at it, impatient with her own weakness.

The coldness of the compress helped her steady herself. When she returned her defiant gaze to him Zandro hadn't moved, standing as though fixed to the floor, watching her.

He shifted then, a slight movement of shoulders, feet, and thrust his hands into his trouser pockets, examining her as if for flaws—she was sure he could find plenty.

Unexpectedly he said, 'You have a case, I suppose—morally, if not legally. There will be conditions, but provided no harm comes to Nicky I'm willing to talk about visiting rights.'

CHAPTER TWO

'*VISITING RIGHTS?*' He would concede his nephew's mother the right to *visit* her child? Such magnanimity.

Swallowing the sarcastic addendum, she reminded herself again that losing her temper would do no good. 'That isn't enough,' she said, with an effort sticking to understatement. 'You can't expect me to accept it.'

'But you expect *me* to tamely hand over Nicky to you—a stranger?'

Her heart jumping with panic and then rage at the callous remark, she made another effort to steady herself. 'His *mother,*' she reiterated. If she repeated the words often enough surely they would seem more real, to herself as well as to him.

Zandro's own anger escaped his iron control. 'You haven't been near him since he was two months old!'

'That's not my fault!' Zandro couldn't have forgotten the promise he'd extracted, made Lia sign her name to. 'You wouldn't *let* me near him!'

'In the state you were in, do you blame me? It was for his sake.'

Did he truly believe that? Had anything more than family pride and possessiveness been behind his insistence that Rico's son had a right to be raised as a Brunellesci and Lia must give him up?

No, she reminded herself. Zandro and his parents could have helped without taking Dominic away. If he'd really had the child's interests in mind he'd have found some way to support its mother, not cut her off from any contact with her son. 'It was a mistake,' she said, 'leaving him with you.'

His look held contempt and disbelief. 'You would take him away from everything—everyone—he knows?'

'I realise I can't uplift him without warning.' She might not know a great deal about children, but that much was basic. 'I hoped you and your parents would be reasonable—allow him time to get used to me before...before I take him home.'

'*This* is his home.' His autocratic tone brooked no argument. 'Where he will stay until he's old enough to decide for himself.'

Moistening her lips, she formed her next words carefully. 'Perhaps your parents will think differently. You don't know how it feels to have a child. Your mother might understand.'

'I know how it feels.'

An unpleasant shock stirred in her stomach. 'You have a child?'

'I have Nicky,' he said. 'And I don't intend to let him go.'

Deadlock. In his rock-hard face she saw the same unyielding willpower he'd exerted in order to get his hands on Dominic, to force through the paperwork that made him the baby's legal guardian, ensuring there could be no comeback if Lia changed her mind.

She wasn't giving up, but banging her head against the brick wall of his intransigence wouldn't accomplish anything at this point. 'I'd like to see him,' she said.

'He'll be having his nap.'

'I'll wait.' Short of bodily throwing her out, or getting a henchman to do it, he wouldn't shift her.

He regarded her consideringly for several seconds,

perhaps weighing how much of a fight she'd put up if he did physically remove her. Then he gave a short, surprised laugh, strode to a discreet intercom on the wall and pressed a button. 'Two cups and a pot of coffee please, Mrs Walker,' he said into the machine. 'And something to eat.'

Switching off, he wandered to a window, looking out at the driveway and lawns. Perhaps realising it was discourteous to present his back to a guest, however unwelcome, he turned abruptly. 'When did you begin watching the house?' he asked.

'Yesterday was the first time.'

'Have you been in Australia for long?'

'Since the day before.'

'Where are you staying?'

She told him, but he didn't seem to recognise the name of the bed and breakfast accommodation. Small, cheap and basic, it was no doubt not the kind of place that he or anyone he knew would even notice. 'It's clean,' she said. 'And quiet.'

He glanced out of the window, then returned his attention to her. 'I tried to keep track of you after you left here. You moved about a lot. I didn't know you'd returned to New Zealand.'

'You had me watched?' Resentment at the intrusion coloured her voice. 'Why?' Had he anticipated that Lia might one day challenge his guardianship of her son? Hoped for some damning sign that would count against her, strengthen his position?

His mouth went tight. 'I wanted to know if you were all right. You're Nicky's mother, after all. And Rico loved you, however wrong-headed he was.'

Rico, his younger brother who had loved life and lived for the moment, impatient with the restrictions and expectations of the Brunellesci family. And who had paid the price and died far too young in the wreckage of his car, leaving a baby and a desperate, injured and grief-stricken mother who couldn't cope with what had happened to her and her child.

Even after securing legal custody of his brother's child, Zandro had been concerned about Lia? Hard to believe.

He might, she supposed, have been protecting the family's reputation, perhaps afraid of what Rico's lover might say about his brother, about his parents, about Zandro himself.

'I managed,' she said. 'My…my friends helped, when I got back home to New Zealand.'

'Better friends, I hope, than the ones you had in Sydney.'

Sydney was where Lia had met Rico, she on a working holiday from New Zealand, he escaping what he'd called the suffocation of his family home and business.

It had been love at first sight; at least that was what they'd believed. One look at Lia and no other woman existed for Rico—he'd told her so on their second meeting. She'd felt exactly the same. The pace of their affair was matched by the pace of their lifestyle—fast, frenetic, sometimes wild. They were young, heedless, caring for nothing but each other, the need to enjoy every moment as if they knew their time would be short, eager to explore every heady new sensation to the fullest. Perhaps deep down they'd known that such sizzling, euphoric emotion couldn't last. But never had Lia dreamed it could end so shatteringly.

When she'd fled back to New Zealand it was to a totally different lifestyle, after finally realising how few people she could rely on once her laughing, handsome lover was dead, his money gone with him, her baby taken and her health broken.

A plump middle-aged woman entered with a tray that she placed on the table nearest the visitor. Noticing the compress as she straightened, the woman looked surprised. 'You're hurt? Can I do anything?'

Zandro looked at the compress. 'Perhaps some more ice, Mrs Walker... Lia?'

'No, it's fine now, but maybe you could take this away?' She unwound the compress, and when the housekeeper had left inquired, 'What happened to Mrs Strickland?'

'She retired and went to live with her daughter in Sydney.' Zandro crossed the big room and poured coffee into the cups, silently indicating the sugar and milk on the tray. He picked up his cup as she added sugar to hers. 'I would like to believe,' he said, straightening with the cup in his hand, 'that you have changed—a lot. Is that possible?'

'What do you think?' she demanded witheringly. 'After losing Rico and having his baby snatched away, you supposed there'd be no change?'

Something flickered across his face, too fast for her to identify it. Chagrin, perhaps—surely not compassion.

It was quickly replaced by an impenetrable mask when he'd seated himself opposite her. 'The fact is, you have no rights now. You agreed, and it was all legal and aboveboard.'

He'd been much smarter than Lia. Taken her to a lawyer—his lawyer—to sign over her baby to him. No doubt the legalese was watertight.

Her jaw ached and she looked down into her coffee, trying not to snap back a retort that would only antagonise him. 'My information,' she said, 'is that a parent can rescind guardianship.'

'Are you prepared to bear the scrutiny of a court on your suitability to care for Nicky?'

Aware of being on frighteningly shaky ground, she gulped some coffee and tried to sound confident. 'If you insist on taking it that far. I have nothing to hide.' A barefaced lie. She told herself—not for the first time—that desperate situations demanded desperate measures. Saving a child from a life of misery surely justified a few unavoidable falsehoods.

'Nothing?' He seemed incredulous, and again she experienced a nervous, dreaded uncertainty.

He couldn't possibly have guessed her secret. His scepticism was based on what little he'd known of Lia months ago, after his brother's death.

If her perilous bluff failed she *would* go to court, tell the truth and throw every resource she could muster into the fight to beat the Brunellescis and take Dominic home where he belonged. A proper home where he'd be loved for himself, not for what he represented to the future of a business empire. A home where love and understanding were more important than money, and success was measured by the quality of relationships and the satisfaction of a job well done, instead of company dividends. Where he'd be allowed to choose his career, rather than be indoctrinated with the idea that as a Brunellesci he was destined to be swallowed up by the corporate politics of the family's various holdings. And where he'd never be forced into a role that would stultify him and break his spirit.

Zandro was staring intently at her. 'A solo mother,' he said, 'with…let's say dubious connections. And have you had a job since you left here?' he pressed.

'Yes.' No need to panic. She didn't have to answer his questions. Pre-empting the next one, she said, 'I don't have a lot of money, but I own a house.' Her parents had left it mortgage-free on their deaths. Just an ordinary three-bedroom suburban bungalow in Auckland, but a house all the same. An asset. Of course she and Dominic couldn't stay there—she'd have to sell it—but she wasn't going to tell Zandro of her long-term plan. 'I can make a good life for Dominic. I'll give up everything to make sure of it.'

'And how long will this altruism last?'

'It isn't altruism. It's love. Maternal instinct.' Boldly she met his eyes.

He made an acid sound of disbelief.

She ignored it. 'You could help make the change-over easy for him.'

He finished his coffee in one gulp and put down the cup, then sat back and folded his arms, seemingly thinking. 'He's happy here, he has everything he needs, and if you're the loving mother you're pretending to be you'll leave him.'

Her heart gave a brief lurch, and she forced herself to breathe normally and stay silent.

'I propose that you visit him as many times as you like while you're here—to satisfy yourself he couldn't be better off.'

He didn't begin to understand her compulsion. A mother's frantic need to rescue a child she felt she'd deserted was only half of it.

He paused. 'And if it works out, we can talk about visiting rights for the future.'

'Visits aren't an adequate substitute for living in the same house.'

Visiting could never equal having Dominic with her,

watching him grow from day to day, putting him to bed each night—all the things that went with parenting.

Maybe Zandro had misunderstood. He said, after a pause, 'I know it's not the same. You want to move in?'

For a moment she didn't comprehend what he was suggesting. Then she blinked. 'You're inviting me here?'

Almost certainly he was ruing it. His face was stiffly set, the angularity of his features more noticeable. 'I'd like to reassure you that your son is in the best hands, and send you home with an easy mind.'

No chance—but she didn't say the words aloud, afraid that he'd retract. Before she'd arrived here she'd told herself that Dominic's material needs, at the very least, would be met. Even kindness would be arranged for, if not freely given. Yet the image had haunted her of a motherless baby, perhaps alone in some empty room of a huge, cold house.

Zandro had said that his nephew didn't lack for affection. But, too young to understand though Dominic had been, surely he must have noticed the sudden absence of his mother, felt abandoned, insecure?

'All right,' she said. And with an effort, 'Thank you.'

She wouldn't be exactly welcome, that much she knew. What would Zandro's parents make of the astounding invitation? Judging by his father's attitude, she could expect to be cold-shouldered if not insulted.

But she hadn't come here to be comfortable. She'd come because Dominic needed her, because this was an obligation she couldn't refuse.

It seemed she'd surprised Zandro yet again. His hands gripped the arms of his chair before he slowly

relaxed them. 'I'll ask my mother to have a room prepared for you,' he said.

She felt a little dazed. Things were moving faster
than she'd expected, although he'd promised nothing
except that he would *not* give up Dominic. Did he really believe she would stay for a while, then pronounce
herself satisfied with his arrangements for his brother's
child, and tamely leave?

He didn't, she decided, have much imagination. But
she wasn't about to point out to him that throwing a
pining mother into close proximity with her stolen
child was unlikely to lead her to abandon it a second
time. 'When shall I come?'

Better strike while the iron was hot, give him no
chance to find some excuse to rescind.

He shrugged, though she fancied it cost him some
effort to appear so nonchalant. 'Give me time to…
inform my parents that you will be staying—for a
while.'

Perhaps she'd imagined the emphasis on the last
phrase. He didn't need to worry. She had no desire to
remain in the Brunellesci household for any longer than
it took her to persuade them that a mother's rights took
precedence over any others.

She fought another twinge of conscience. By
Zandro's own admission his mother was too old and
he was too busy to give Dominic undivided attention.
While Domenico apparently took some distant interest
in his grandson, no doubt he left practical matters of
child care to his wife and the nanny.

No matter what they thought, a paid employee
couldn't give the same unstinting devotion to Dominic
she could. He was all she had in the world now.

Grief threatened to overwhelm her and she turned

her head, pretending to admire a large oil colour on the wall, a luminous study of a young girl in a white dress, perched on a chair before a window where gauzy curtains floated on an invisible breeze.

It didn't really help, so she put down the coffee cup she'd emptied and stood up. 'I'll go then,' she said, 'and pack my things.' It wouldn't take long. Not a naturally pushy person, nevertheless she was determined not to let him back out. 'I hired a car in town... Can I garage it here—or will I need it? I don't suppose I'll be going out much.' And if she did, she could use public transport now there was no need for discreet surveillance.

He said, 'Return it. I'll send a car for you tonight.' And after a slight hesitation, 'About seven. You may join us for dinner.'

Gracious of him, she thought snidely, but bit back the urge to say it aloud. He probably wasn't looking forward to breaking the news to his father that someone Domenico had called *that woman*—and, she suspected, something much worse—was about to invade his home.

She wondered if the old man might veto the idea and countermand his son.

Evidently if there had been objections Zandro had overridden them. The car arrived promptly—one of a fleet that specialised in corporate business, according to the logo on the side.

When they reached the Brunellesci house the driver spoke into the microphone, and in response the gates opened. He drove to the stone steps, where the door was opened by the housekeeper.

As the driver lifted the single suitcase out of the boot

and set it on the verandah, Zandro's deep voice said, 'I'll take care of that, Mrs Walker.'

He came forward, flicking a critical glance over their guest, evidently noting that she'd changed into a cool cotton dress worn with wedge-heeled sandals.

His greeting was coldly polite. 'Good evening, Lia. Mrs Walker will take you upstairs. I'll bring your case in a few minutes.' He turned to speak to the driver.

The woman showed her to a large bedroom with embossed creamy-gold wallpaper, dimmed by trees outside that grew taller than the house. A bronze satin spread covered the queen-size bed. The adjoining bathroom was green-tiled and gleamed with gold fittings.

Mrs Walker left before Zandro arrived with her case, putting it down on a blanket box at the foot of the bed. 'Do you have everything you need?' he inquired.

'Thank you. Yes, I think so.' She too could be polite but not friendly.

'You know your way to the dining room. We'll be sitting down in about twenty minutes.' He cast her a searching look. 'If you'd like a drink first we're in the front room.'

'I'll be down soon,' she promised. 'I'd like a gin and tonic if you have it.'

He inclined his head slightly in acknowledgement before leaving.

She crossed the room to close the door behind him and leaned back against it, letting out a long breath. Zandro Brunellesci was not a man she could comfortably be in the same room with. Every time he came within touching distance she could feel the force of his personality, an aura of power, determination and authority, making her nerves skitter all over the place.

Staying in the same house with Dominic meant living with Zandro and his disquieting effect on her.

Moving away from the door, she caught a glimpse of herself in the mirror over the big dressing table. She looked apprehensive, her cheeks flushed with colour, eyes dark in the middle, the pupils enlarged, the green irises softened to almost grey.

She squared her shoulders, trying to banish the look. Sure, Zandro was intimidating, but she'd known that all along. Known too that she could—*must*—stand up to whatever obstacles he put in the way of her plans. And never let him know on what shaky foundations those plans actually rested.

One step at a time. The first was to go downstairs and face the enemy. The three faces of the Brunellesci family, ranged against her.

CHAPTER THREE

THE front room, Zandro had said. She followed the sound of voices to a door that stood ajar. The first face she saw on entering the big room was his. He was standing, talking with his father. Looking over the older man's shoulder, he found her eyes, abruptly falling silent.

Domenico turned, his fierce gaze lighting on her as she paused in the doorway. She saw his hand tighten on the cane he held, then he drew himself up to his considerable height and gave her a curt nod. 'Good evening, Lia.'

Walking into the room, she returned the greeting in a steady voice. Then she saw a motherly figure encased in floral silk, her greying hair pulled into a bun, ensconced on a sofa with Dominic snuggled into the angle of a comfortable lap.

The old woman looked up, her eyes wary, perhaps anxious. '*Buona sera*, Lia.'

Dominic wore some kind of one-piece pyjama suit, yellow and printed with teddy bears. Black curls covered his head, and his mouth was like a pink rosebud. Round, dark eyes regarded this new person with curiosity, and she took a couple of quick steps towards him, her arms lifting.

He turned from her and buried his face in his grandmother's bosom, one tiny hand clutching at the shiny silk, roundly rejecting the overture.

35

Letting her hands fall, she felt exposed, and at a loss what to do.

Then Zandro was at her side, holding out a glass to her, his eyes commanding, willing her to take it. 'Your gin and tonic,' he said. 'Drink it.'

His voice was low, with a rough edge. He took her arm and led her to a couch, where she wrapped both her hands about the glass he had pressed on her. It was cold, ice clinking as her hands trembled.

Of course Dominic didn't recognise her. Her head knew that but unthinking instinct, the primal tug of a bond he couldn't be expected to sense, and which had taken her unawares, had led her to make that futile gesture.

Zandro didn't say *I told you so*. He sipped from his beer and told her, 'Nicky's often shy with new people at first. But curiosity will get the better of him.'

As if to reinforce the remark, the baby turned his head until one eye could find her. When he saw her looking back at him he immediately hid his face again.

Zandro laughed, but she didn't join in. Her throat hurt too much.

She hadn't known she would feel such emotion, like a warm flood tide. Children had been something she'd vaguely looked forward to in the future, before she found out about Dominic. The sensation on finally being confronted with a living, breathing baby had been something of a shock. He'd instantly become a person—a tiny person who was her responsibility. Someone she must love and care for.

Again she vowed to do that, to make any sacrifice he needed from her.

Mrs Brunellesci was looking down at him, stroking

a heavily veined hand over the soft curls, murmuring something to him in Italian.

She loves him.

The thought was like a cold shower. She ought to be glad, even grateful. If Zandro saw Dominic as a responsibility, an obligation, and the old man regarded a grandson as some kind of insurance for the future of his company, at least one member of the family had given the baby genuine affection. And he loved, trusted his grandmother.

But I have to take him away.

Doubt entered her mind, whispering like a malevolent goblin. *Is it fair? Can you do that to him—to her? Should you?* Her stomach made a sickening revolution.

The gin was blessedly steadying. Zandro had been quite heavy-handed with it, light on the tonic.

Mrs Brunellesci asked in a heavily accented voice, 'Your room, is all right, Lia?'

Trying to smile, she said, 'Yes, fine. Thank you for letting me stay.'

'Zandro says you wish to know your son. He says you have a right.'

He did? Her gaze went involuntarily to him. Again she could feel that indefinable masculine charge that seemed to hum around him.

A muffled thump drew her attention to his father. Domenic stood scowling, leaning on his stick with both hands, and as she watched he lifted it a little and brought it down again with another thump.

Zandro got up. 'Please sit, Papa, and I'll get you another drink,' he offered, guiding his father to a chair.

Domenico shook him off, saying something explosive in Italian before sinking into the armchair.

Apparently unruffled, Zandro grinned, and fetched a

glass of rich red wine for his father, who accepted it with a grunt and continued to scowl while he drank it.

Zandro didn't sit down again, prowling about the room while he finished off his beer, then placing the empty glass on the drinks cabinet.

Dominic lifted his head at last from his grandmother's protection and looked around. He wriggled down from her lap, sliding to the floor, and then on hands and knees made a beeline for his uncle.

Zandro bent as the baby drew near, picked him up and swung him high, big hands firmly holding the little boy's body under his gleefully waving arms. Dominic giggled, and Zandro smiled up at him. He lowered the child into his arms and unselfconsciously kissed a fat cheek.

It was astonishing. Nothing in what he'd said had hinted at genuine fond feelings for his nephew.

Dominic raised a hand to pat his uncle's face, poking a finger into his mouth. Zandro growled, pretending to relish the finger, making smacking noises with his lips, and again the baby giggles pealed.

This wasn't as she'd assumed it would be. She felt oddly panicky.

Zandro, the baby still in his arms, strolled over to her, taking his time. He sat beside her, settling Dominic on his knees.

The baby stared solemnly at the other occupant of the sofa and Zandro said softly, 'Nicky—this is your mother.'

'Ma?' He turned to his uncle again.

'Mother,' Zandro said. 'Mo-ther. Mamma.'

'Ma-ma.' Dominic giggled some more, then struggled upright to stand on the man's knees, exploring his

face with inquisitive fingers. He lost his balance and
Zandro caught him, settling him again.

This time the little boy regarded the strange woman
for longer, and finally stretched out a hand. She lifted
her own and he curled his around two fingers with a
surprisingly strong grip. Something happened to her
heart—as if those baby fingers had squeezed it too.

The nanny appeared in the doorway and briskly entered the room. 'Time for bed?' she said, spying her
charge, and Dominic dropped the fingers he held, wriggled from Zandro's hold and took off towards his
grandmother.

The nanny snatched him into her arms, laughing, and
held him while Mrs Brunellesci gave him a kiss, then
Domenic did the same.

Zandro stood up as they approached him. 'Barbara,'
he said, 'this is Lia Cameron, Nicky's mother. Barbara
Ayreshire, Lia.'

The woman looked only slightly surprised, perhaps
already forewarned. 'Hello.' She smiled. 'He's a bonny
boy, isn't he?'

'Yes.' Impossible to say any more, although she
ought to congratulate the woman on how well Dominic
had been looked after, tell her she was pleased, thankful.

But she couldn't do it. Rage and resentment surfaced. It wouldn't be fair to take it out on Barbara, who
was only doing—and doing well—a job that she was
paid for. A job that should have been done for nothing
but love, by Dominic's own mother.

Barbara Ayreshire joined them as they sat down to
dinner, placing a baby monitor on the long sideboard.
She was at Domenic's right, beside Zandro, while the

elder Brunellescis took the head and foot of the table. Which left a chair on Domenic's left for Lia.

She was conscious throughout the meal of the old man's unbending demeanour, although he poured wine for her and passed her butter and salt; and of Zandro sitting opposite her, his nearly black eyes enigmatic when they clashed with hers and held them for moments at a time.

Refusing to lower her gaze, to meekly accept she was an unwelcome spectre at the feast and pretend she wasn't even there, she stared back at him each time until someone claimed his attention, or the housekeeper laid another dish in front of him and he turned to thank her.

Mrs Brunellesci occasionally addressed a remark to Lia in her richly accented English. Had she had a good flight from New Zealand? What was the weather like there? How much was the time difference?

Poor woman, she was doing her best. It was a relief to turn to her and try to conduct an ordinary conversation.

The nanny inquired which part of New Zealand their visitor was from—oh, Auckland? Barbara had visited the city, also some tourist spots—Rotorua's boiling springs and the equally popular Bay of Islands in the north. 'What a beautiful country it is.'

Even Zandro spoke to her several times, concurring with Barbara's opinion, asking if Lia needed sauce for her dessert, commenting that one of the cheeses presented after that was from New Zealand. He sliced off a piece, holding it out to her on the cheese knife.

She took it because it would look ungracious if she didn't, placed it on a cracker and nibbled until it was gone. But surely they were all glad when the meal was over.

Coffee was served in the front room. While the others sat down, Barbara took her cup and excused herself, leaving with it in her hand. It would have been nice to follow suit.

'Lia?' Zandro stood before her, handing her a cup. 'I've sugared it for you.'

'Thank you.' He'd remembered how she liked her coffee. That should perhaps have made her feel less alienated. Instead she was bothered. He was too observant, those gleaming impenetrable eyes not missing anything. And too often they were fixed on her as if trying to gauge her thoughts, delve into her deepest secrets.

Of which she had at least one too many. If he found her out she had no doubt there would be hell to pay.

She drank her coffee quickly and stood up. 'If you'll excuse me…'

'You must be tired.' Mrs Brunellesci's understanding nod failed to hide her relief. 'It's two hours later in New Zealand, you said?'

Zandro came to the door with her. 'Goodnight, Lia. If you need anything Mrs Walker will take care of it.'

She wouldn't have dreamed of disturbing the housekeeper, but she nodded and said, 'Thank you.'

Going up the stairs, a faint tingling along her spine convinced her that his too-perceptive gaze was still on her. It took an effort not to look back when she got to the top, to keep walking until she reached the relative safety of her room.

She wasn't going to be cowed by him, or anyone.

Which room, she wondered, had they assigned to Nicky? Already she'd begun to use the family's diminutive. It had jarred at first that he bore a nickname unknown to his own mother. But it suited him, the name he'd been given for his grandfather's sake too burdensome for such a small person. Perhaps in time he would grow into it…and become as insensitive and judgmental as the other males in the household?

'Not if I can help it!' The words, spoken aloud, echoed in the big room. Despite the heat outside, she shivered. Tonight Rico's family had been indulgent towards their youngest member, even tender and loving. Babies could be allowed to be babies. But when he became a young boy and then a man, wouldn't he inevitably suffer as Rico had, relentlessly pressured into the family mould, bullied and browbeaten until he either knuckled down and accepted his fate, or rebelled?

Rico had rebelled, but the shadow of his family had always been there during his all-too-short time with Lia, when the two of them had lived in their own closed, defensive world.

Zandro had intruded in person on that world, breaching the cocoon they'd made for themselves. He'd looked at Lia with contempt, scarcely acknowledging her existence, and talked to his brother about family honour, about obligations, about their parents' disappointment at Rico's 'ruining his life.' About a place being ready for him whenever he came to his senses and returned to his home and family. And the sooner that happened the better.

'It's emotional blackmail!' Lia had said later. 'Don't listen to him. He's trying to make you feel guilty, manipulate you.' She couldn't believe Zandro had any feelings of his own. His eyes had been frosty, his expression barely hiding distaste—for her, and for the small flat that she and Rico shared, so different from the palatial home Rico had fled and swore he'd never go back to. And for the lifestyle they'd chosen, living for the day.

It had been, no doubt, feckless and irresponsible. Zandro had certainly thought so. He'd warned that Rico's generous allowance could be cut off if he persisted in 'this idiocy.' Lia was convinced he was taking a perverse pleasure in the threat.

She'd made some sound of protest, clutched Rico's arm to support him in his defiance, and Zandro had turned his inimical gaze on her, his lips curling in a way that made her cringe. 'Your girlfriend,' he'd said, looking at Lia but speaking to his brother, 'wouldn't like that. Do you think she'll stick around when you have no money?' Making it obvious that he thought he knew the answer…

That was when Rico had told him to go. For once standing up to his older brother. Defending Lia.

Breakfast, Mrs Walker had said, rattling off information that she was obviously accustomed to giving guests on their arrival, was served at seven-thirty. 'Before Mr Zandro goes off to the office. But I can do something for you later if you like.'

'No, that's fine.' Putting an extra burden on the household help would be inconsiderate. And although here under sufferance, inevitably she would come face-to-face with the family sometime during the day. Was Nicky allowed at the breakfast table?

With five minutes to spare she left her room and was arrested by the murmur of Barbara Ayreshire's voice from one of the other rooms along the passageway, and Nicky's incomprehensible burble.

Turning away from the stairs, she followed the brass-edged carpet runner to the source of the sound, finding a half-open door and pushing it wider.

A blue cot with rumpled bedclothes occupied one corner of the room. Above it a clown mobile hung, and the ceiling was blue too, with painted animals peeking from behind misty clouds.

The nanny stood before a changing table near the cot, obscuring the baby. When she picked him up he looked over her shoulder directly at the doorway. 'Duh!' he said, pointing.

The woman turned to the newcomer. 'Oh, good morning, Ms Cameron.'

'Good morning.' Her eyes were on the baby. 'Please, call me Lia.' She hoped it sounded casual, friendly. The trusting way the baby snuggled close to the nanny evoked an unfamiliar emotion. One pudgy hand was clutching at the white collar of the woman's polka-dotted pale pink dress, his cheek resting on her shoulder.

'Would he come to me?' she couldn't resist asking, walking forward slowly so as not to alarm the child.

'I don't know. He might remember you from last night.'

This time there was no audience except the nanny to see if he rebuffed her. She held out her arms, said quietly, 'Nicky?'

He turned to look up at Barbara, who gave him an encouraging smile. 'That's your mummy,' she said, earning for herself, although she couldn't know it, a rush of gratitude. 'Do you want to give her a cuddle?'

The little boy looked back at the inviting arms extended to him, then stretched out his own, and the nanny relinquished him.

He was surprisingly heavy, curving into her careful

embrace. Warm, and smelling of shampoo and baby powder and…baby, she realised, inhaling the sweet, clean scent. He leaned against her breasts and took a fistful of her hair, gazing at her with gravity, as if trying to memorise her features.

Maybe a subconscious part of his baby mind recognised them from an earlier time. Did she seem dimly familiar to him after all? And surely a trace of likeness to her own face was discernible in his?

Then he smiled, a wide grin making several small white teeth visible, and she felt tears pricking the back of her eyes. Memories both happy and sad floated through her mind.

He was a lovely baby, and it wasn't fair that he'd been deprived of his mother, that she'd missed out on the changes of the last ten months, not had the pleasure of seeing his first real smile, hearing his first laugh, discovering his first tooth, watching him learn to crawl as he did so efficiently now. Missed, too, his birthday, by several weeks.

Who were the Brunellescis to decide that a child was better off without his mother? Lia might have been inexperienced and penniless, but the first she could have overcome, and the second had been well within their power to correct, for the baby's sake.

Instead they'd taken him away from her. Left her to fend for herself as best she could.

That wasn't love, it was an exercise of naked power.

The baby tugged at the strand of hair he held, and Barbara said, 'Careful, Nicky!'

'It's all right.' Gently unwinding the clinging fingers, holding the warm little hand in her own, smiling forgiveness, she couldn't resist kissing a smooth, rounded cheek.

Nicky ducked and then gave her a mischievous grin, a sly sideways glance. He presented his cheek to her and when she puckered her lips dodged again, making her laugh. It was a game he obviously enjoyed.

'Little tease,' Barbara said cheerfully. 'He'll give the girls a hard time when he grows up.' She checked her watch. 'Are you going down for breakfast?'

'Yes, I was. Are you?'

'Nicky and I have ours in the kitchen. His table manners leave something to be desired—don't they, young man?' Deftly the nanny removed the baby to her own arms.

So he wasn't tolerated at the family table? Banished because he might make a mess and spoil their coldly formal meals? It was tempting to ask, *Can't I join you?* That would be a lot more comfortable than eating with the grown-ups. But she supposed if she offended the elder Brunellescis it wouldn't help her case.

When she went down the three of them were already seated in a glass-walled conservatory off the dining room, reached by a shallow flight of steps. Plants hung on the walls, and the round marble table was ringed by four white-painted cane chairs with padded fabric seats. Another two chairs had been put aside in a corner. A tea trolley held cereal, bread, salami and cheese, a pot of jam and one of honey.

'I'm sorry if I'm late,' she said. Zandro rose from his chair and pulled one out for her, offered coffee from a pot on the trolley. As she took the chair, Domenico lowered the newspaper he was reading, nodded his patrician head and raised the paper again.

His wife looked apologetic. '*Buon giorno,* Lia.'

Zandro poured her coffee. 'Did you sleep well?' His voice was coolly courteous. Making conversation but not as if he really cared. He sat down again and passed the sugar bowl over as she murmured, 'Yes, thank you.'

'If you would like toast or a cooked breakfast—'

'I'm not very hungry first thing in the morning.' She reached for the corn flakes on the trolley, shook some into the bowl before her and picked up the white china jug to pour milk on them. Her hand, she noted, pleased with her composure, was steady.

His eyes inspected her, taking a leisurely but dispassionate inventory of her upper body. 'You were very thin...before.'

Mrs Brunellesci said unexpectedly, 'Too skinny. Domenico!' She turned to her husband and he lowered his paper again. 'Lia looks good now, you think? More healthy. A woman should look like a woman, is what you say, hey?'

He directed an icy, reluctant stare across the table. 'Better,' he agreed, before folding the paper noisily and laying it aside to take up a cup of coffee.

Zandro's mouth twitched, a muscle moving near his jawbone. He was trying not to laugh.

That the man had a sense of humour at all was a revelation. And the fact that he could find his father amusing was a kind of comfort, making Domenico seem less formidable.

Zandro caught her eye and his mouth straightened.

This time she looked away first, chilled by the sudden change in his expression to an aloofness that almost matched the older man's. As Rico had said, they were cut from the same pattern. Both of them cared more for the business and the family name than for anything. And to preserve and protect those two things they would sacrifice anyone and anything else—Rico, Rico's son... She mustn't let herself be swayed by their apparent fondness for Nicky, an indulgence that almost certainly would not outlast his babyhood.

She spooned up some corn flakes and began to eat.

Zandro left the table first, she supposed to go to his city office. Not long afterwards, as she excused herself and rose from her chair, she heard the car leave the garage, glimpsed it moving through the gateway.

Her bed had been made while she was at breakfast. Unused to being waited on, she made a mental note to make it herself tomorrow before she went down. And she'd find out from Mrs Walker when the sheets were changed, and where the clean linen was kept.

She heard muted footfalls on the carpet and glanced through the open doorway to see Barbara passing. Calling the woman's name, she hurried to the hallway. 'Where's Nicky?'

'With his grandmother,' Barbara replied. 'This is their time, while I tidy our rooms. Later we'll go to the park.' She paused, then said tentatively, 'You might like to come with us?'

There was no way the nanny could have missed the chill in the air since her charge's mother had appeared out of the blue, though she might not have been told she could lose her job. Still, she seemed a nice woman. Perhaps here was an ally, someone who might help soften the old man's hard heart.

No opportunity should be rejected, even if the thought of accompanying Mr Brunellesci on his morning jaunt was a daunting one. *It can't be so bad. What could he do to you?*

Apart from ignoring her, nothing much. She took a breath. 'Thank you, I'd like that.'

'Ten o'clock, then. We'll see you downstairs.'

*   *   *

She joined them just before ten. Barbara was strapping Nicky into his pushchair, and straightened to say, 'Mr Brunellesci isn't coming today.'

Was the old man sulking? 'Is he angry with you for inviting me along? I hope you're not in trouble.'

Barbara said tranquilly, 'I'm not in any trouble. Bruce will be with us—Mrs Walker's husband. He does the gardening and odd jobs about the place. Shall we go?'

She sounded brisk and her voice didn't suggest this was anything out of the ordinary, but she was avoiding eye contact. It wasn't difficult to deduce she was embarrassed.

They descended the steps and were joined by a burly man wearing a plaid shirt, jeans and boots. 'Bruce,' the nanny said to him, 'this is…'

'Lia,' she supplied firmly as Barbara hesitated. 'I'm Nicky's mother.' His wife had probably told him about her already and he showed no surprise, merely nodding and saying, 'Hello,' before he preceded them to the gates.

The world outside the walls seemed noisy and vast— the sky arching high, the ocean stretching to infinity, the intermittent cars on the road snarling past.

At the park Barbara lifted Nicky into the swing and pushed him a few times, then offered, 'Would you like to take a turn, Lia?'

'I'd love to.' She stood in front of the swing, wanting to see his face as he sailed back and forth, anxious not to overdo it and frighten him.

He kicked his legs and grunted impatiently, and Barbara said, 'He wants to go higher.'

A harder push, and Dominic's face lit up with sheer

joy. His eyes were bright and clear, his cheeks flushed, and his infectious giggle made her smile, laugh back at him.

It seemed a long time since she had really laughed.

They went down to the beach, Nicky holding both the women's hands as he paddled in the shallow wavelets that foamed about his toes, encased in plastic sandals.

Then they swung him up the beach between them, distracting him from his wish, expressed with loud howls, to stay in the water and go deeper.

'You can swim in your paddling pool later,' Barbara told him. 'One, two, three—whee!' He flew briefly through the air with his fingers firmly wrapped in the women's hands, apparently forgetting the appeal of the water in this other delightful experience.

Barbara took off his sandals, brushed sand from his feet and dried them on a small towel, then played Piggy Went to Market with his toes before starting to put his sandals back on.

'I suppose he needs those?' There were snakes in Australia, and poisonous spiders, perhaps other nasties that New Zealanders weren't bothered by.

Barbara looked up from buckling Nicky's sandal onto a wriggling foot. 'The Brunellescis are very careful. They want to keep him safe.'

'Is that why Bruce is here?' The man was sitting on one of the seats a few metres away looking bored, muscular arms crossed. 'Do they think I might kidnap Nicky?'

'I don't know what they think. Zandro said you want to get to know Nicky. He asked what I thought about it.'

'He did?' Surprising that Zandro cared for any opinion other than his own—but then, Barbara was his hired expert. It was logical to consult her. 'What did you say?'

Barbara had closed one buckle and captured Nicky's other foot. 'I said I approved. I've seen enough uncaring parents—with a few exceptions I think contact should be encouraged.'

'Thank you!'

'Every child has a right to know its mother. No one can really take her place.'

Seeming to come to a decision as she stood up, Barbara said frankly, 'I have strict instructions not to leave him alone with anyone but his grandparents or his uncle, and if Mr Brunellesci or Zandro aren't available, to take Bruce with us when we're out.' Her brown eyes might have held sympathy. 'I'm sure they have Nicky's welfare at heart.'

Maybe they don't have hearts. Not normal, human ones. Maybe it's a congenital condition the Brunellescis are born with. Only Rico had escaped it.

But when Zandro picked up his nephew last night, and when Domenico kissed him goodnight, it had contradicted her perception of them as cold, arrogant despots. The scene had not fitted with all she knew of them.

It made little difference, she told herself. Babies did disarm people. Helpless and appealing, they survived because human beings were programmed to respond to that and protect them until they could fend for themselves. If the Brunellescis were capable of love, it was a kind of love that could become repressive, as it had with Rico.

While Nicky napped she retreated to her room, examining the dozen or so books that occupied a shelf under the bedside table—a mixture of classic fiction and modern thrillers with a couple on travel in exotic places. She flicked through an account of a trip through India, Kathmandu and Tibet, while half her mind was occupied with various scenarios wherein she fulfilled her undertaking and took Nicky home.

Uncertainty fluttered in her stomach, but she couldn't allow it to take over. Remembering what Rico had said about his family, and how ruthlessly they had separated a child from its mother and excluded her from Nicky's life, she bolstered her wavering resolve.

Any thought that Zandro had invited her to stay because he felt some remorse or compunction about his earlier high-handed actions was surely misplaced. He didn't trust her, and he wanted her where he and his father and his henchman could keep an eye on her.

She found a pocket Italian-English dictionary among the books, and tried to recall the word Domenico had used about her...something beginning with *C,* she thought. Running down the page she lighted on it— *cagna.* Bitch.

A strong word for such a gentlemanly old man.

After lunch, at which Domenico did not appear, she spent time with Nicky and Barbara in the garden while Mrs Brunellesci rested in her room. There was a swimming pool enclosed in a child-proof fence, plus a plastic paddling pool. Nicky splashed about happily, accompanied by a flotilla of plastic toys.

When he finally tired of that, he busied himself in the garden, finding endless interest in a single daisy, a fluttering, nondescript grey moth, a fallen leaf. He loved the birds that flashed red, green, yellow, blue among the trees, pointing and clapping his hands, and seemed to enjoy introducing the visitor to the delights of his world.

Later he was taken off for a nap, and Mrs Brunellesci came out to sit under a sun umbrella on a tiled patio near the house, a piece of needlework in her hands.

'Lia,' she beckoned. 'Sit down. Would you like something to drink? The sun is quite hot today, even though it's not summer yet.'

'No, thank you. I'll get myself something if I need it. Did you have a nice sleep?' This woman was her best chance of influencing the old man and his son. At the moment Domenico was the most overtly hostile, although she suspected that Zandro would in the end be the more intransigent, less likely to be swayed by his mother.

Mrs Brunellesci said, 'I rested, not slept.' Her brows drew together over anxious dark eyes remarkably like her elder son's.

Perhaps she'd been thinking about the stranger in their midst, worrying what might come of this visitation.

After sorting through a small box of coloured silks, Mrs Brunellesci chose a bright red thread and snipped off a length. She slipped a pair of glasses onto her nose, sighing. 'Getting old is a pest,' she said. 'My Domenico, it makes him angry.'

'I suspect a lot of things make him angry.' Not a wise thing to say, she really must watch her tongue. 'I'm sorry, I didn't mean—'

The older woman looked up again, sharply, then laughter danced in her eyes and creased her face. She chuckled, a deep, rich sound. 'This is true,' she said. 'Yes, he has a temper, that man.'

She sounded rather proud of him, indulgent. Obvi-

ously she didn't feel her husband's temper was anything to be terribly upset about.

Mrs Brunellesci began stitching, her head bent over
the work. 'Perhaps,' she said, sobering, 'if Domenico
had held on to his temper my Rico would not have left
us. Perhaps he would not have…'

Died. The dread word hung in the air.

'I'm sorry.' What could one say to a mother who
was still grieving for her younger son, her baby?

A shoulder lifted. The needle flashed in and out of
the fabric. 'He broke his mother's heart,' Mrs
Brunellesci said. 'But a mother always loves.'

'Yes.'

The needle faltered. Again the older woman raised
her eyes. She looked troubled. 'We love our Nico—
Nicky,' she said. 'He is looked after, yes? We care very
much for him.'

'I know.' But they'd loved Rico too, yet her husband, aided by Zandro, had driven him out of his home,
away from his family, because their love was blink-
ered, limited, not the unconditional kind that Mrs
Brunellesci had given him and now gave to Nicky.

And if she hadn't stood up to them then, what chance
would she have now that she was older and frailer, and
Zandro was in his prime and following his father's
path? 'I love Nicky too.'

True, despite the relatively little time she'd spent
with him. The bond of blood was a mysterious force,
something both natural and inexplicable. She wished
her own mother and father could have seen their grandchild, held him, known that their genes would live on
in him even after their deaths.

But those deaths had come too soon, like Rico's.
They hadn't been as young as he, but were still too

young to die, victims of a drunken lout who had run them off the road and into a river where they'd drowned while he sped off, not even attempting to help them.

Lia had held herself together through her parents' funeral and the inquest and the harrowing trial of the guilty driver. And she had survived through the several months following. But she'd begun drinking regularly, drinking too much. With the wrong people, and at the wrong times.

Her work had suffered, and eventually she'd been sacked from the job she loved as a travel agent.

Ashamed of herself, she'd made the effort of will to give up alcohol, and decided to start over somewhere else. Australia was nearest.

Using the modest inheritance her parents had left to her she booked a flight, settled in a cramped though outrageously expensive flat in Sydney, and started looking for a job. And met Rico.

'Rico.' His mother sighed again, shook her head. 'He was beautiful, like his son. Happy, always laughing, laughing, when he was a little boy.' She lifted a hand, caught a tear on her finger. Smiled wistfully. 'Ah, my Rico. You loved him too, Lia?'

It was a question, a plea for reassurance that when he left his home, his family, his mother, someone had cared for him. Someone had loved him.

'I did.' It was the only answer she could make, despite the sinking misgiving in her stomach, the suspicion that she was being drawn into murky waters with hidden hazards. With all the sincerity she could infuse into her voice, she said, 'I loved him with all my heart.'

CHAPTER FOUR

A soft sound like a hiss made her look up.

Her startled eyes met Zandro's as he stepped onto the patio. His were very black, with an angry light in them, and his lips were curled in something resembling a snarl, revealing a glimpse of white teeth. The sound she'd heard was his breath drawn between them.

Mrs Brunellesci smiled. 'Zandro! You're home early.'

'Yes, Mamma.' His expression changed as he bent and kissed his mother.

She raised a hand and caressed his hard cheek before he drew back.

'Lia.' He nodded a greeting. His eyes were cold now, watching her consideringly.

She tried to smile, her lips stiff. 'Hello, Zandro.'

He pulled out a chair and sat between the two women. 'Mrs Walker's bringing cool drinks. She told me you were out here.' He studied his mother's handiwork for a couple of seconds, then turned his head to ask, 'You've spent some time with Nicky, Lia?'

'We went to the park this morning with Barbara.' She glanced at Mrs Brunellesci, who was concentrating again on her work, and said defiantly, 'You've no need to set a bodyguard over him.'

He didn't even blink. 'It's my duty to protect the boy.'

Heat singed her cheeks. 'He's perfectly safe with me!'

Mrs Brunellesci was looking in a worried way from one to the other of them, her needlework dropped into her lap. She said, 'Zandro is doing his best for Nicky, Lia. Try to understand.'

'I'm trying,' she said tightly. It would do no good to lose control. Any sign of instability could be used against her, she was sure. 'But I object to being treated like a criminal.'

Zandro said in a mild tone that only made her simmering temper rise, 'If I were treating you like a criminal I would have called the police when I first discovered you spying on my family.'

'*Your* family? Dominic's *mine,*' she said fiercely, reverting to his full name, the one Rico had oddly insisted on despite his estrangement from his father. 'And I wasn't spying!'

'I don't know what else you'd call it,' he said coolly. 'Lurking about in the street, watching.'

'I just wanted to be sure he was here, and all right.'

'I hope you've satisfied yourself of that.'

Did he expect her to up sticks and go now that she knew the baby was healthy and happy—so far? Stiffening, she said, 'I've only been here one day. Anyway, it's his future wellbeing I'm concerned with.'

'As I am.' His soft tone held a note of iron. She saw the remorseless purpose in his face, and inwardly shivered. 'Just because you've suddenly taken a whim to have him back—'

'It isn't a whim!' Her hands clenched into fists in her lap. It would have relieved her feelings to jump up and hit him. 'I'm entitled—'

Zandro didn't let her finish. 'You're entitled to know that he's safe and well.' His voice was harsh. 'Even though you've shown precious little interest until now.

I figured you'd probably forgotten you ever had a child.'

The cutting remark made her shiver, a heavy knot forming in her chest. 'That's not so,' she said huskily. 'I was sick. It wasn't until…until I was well again that I realised what a terrible thing you'd made…made me do.'

'Sick.' The flat monosyllable denoted disbelief. 'Sure.'

Rage banished every other emotion but a lingering grief. 'You have no idea!' she flashed at him, pushing back her chair and standing up. She had to get out of here before she gave herself away, shrieked the truth at him, threw it in his arrogant face. Told him what untold misery and agony he and his father were responsible for. That if they'd left Rico alone he might not have died. And his child could have been brought up by its own mother and father, not in luxury but in love.

She turned away blindly, knowing she mustn't be goaded into saying things she would regret. Things that might arouse suspicion. Zandro wasn't stupid, and if she let something slip he'd be on to it like a tiger on its prey.

Not seeing Mrs Walker coming from the house with a tray of tall glasses holding fresh orange juice, she blundered into the woman, and icy liquid spilled down her loose blouse, making her gasp. Two glasses smashed on the tiles.

'I'm so sorry!' She stepped back, dismayed. The startled housekeeper still held the tray, but yellow juice was spreading over it, dripping to the patio. 'I'll help you clean it up.'

But even as she bent to retrieve some of the broken

shards a hard masculine hand closed about her arm and pulled her back from the mess. 'Don't touch any of that with bare hands,' Zandro said. His glance took in the soaked and stained blouse. 'You'd better go inside and get changed. I'll help Mrs Walker.'

The housekeeper smiled at her. 'It was just a silly accident. You go and get cleaned up, but watch your feet on that glass.'

Zandro still had hold of her arm and, as always when he touched her, she could feel tingles of disconcerting sensation spreading throughout her body. He steered her around the spilled juice and broken glass to the house.

It seemed dark, coming in out of the sunshine. He was a black, bulky shape beside her. 'Are you all right?' he asked, releasing her.

'I wasn't hurt. And I should help—it was my fault.'

'Don't worry about it.' He gave her a little push towards the stairs, and when she glanced back he'd gone.

In her room she stripped off her clothes and put them in the wide basin in the bathroom to soak in cold water. Even her bra was wet. She stepped into the shower, rinsed off the sticky juice, then wrapped one of the big bath towels around her and went back to the bedroom.

She was getting a clean bra from a drawer when someone tapped on the door.

'Who is it?' she called.

It was Mrs Walker, offering to take her clothes for washing.

'I'm soaking them in the bathroom. I can take care of them myself, thank you, if you'll tell me where the laundry is.'

'Well,' the woman said, 'if that's what you prefer,

but it's no trouble, really. I wash twice a week anyway. All you need to do normally is put your things in the basket in the bathroom.'

'Thank you, I'll remember that.' What must it be like, she wondered as the housekeeper left, to be waited on hand and foot all your life? Could it be good for a child?

Quickly she pulled on undies and a cool, cleverly cut loose dress that skimmed her breasts and hips and flared over her knees. Not wanting to confront Zandro again immediately, she stood at the window and stared out over the shorn grass and beautifully kept gardens, the trees that shaded the house from the fierce sun in summer. Outside and in, the place was immaculately, expensively cared for. Just as Nicky was.

Certainly she couldn't afford to give him the material things that his father's family could.

But Rico had turned his back on that family, hadn't wanted Nicky to be reared within it. She could give Rico's son—as she'd promised—love, a wholehearted commitment to his welfare, and a good education. That would cost, but it shouldn't be too difficult if she worked towards it from the start.

Because she didn't intend to take any help from the Brunellescis. The plan was to disappear with the child as soon as she got back to New Zealand and never contact them again. It was the only way she could possibly get away with this outrageous charade.

A hole seemed to have opened just below her ribs. Again she recalled Nicky snuggling into his grandmother's arms, hiding his face in her bosom, and his peals of laughter as Zandro held him aloft, the rigid angles of the man's handsome face breaking into a smile. Even Domenico tenderly kissing his grandson goodnight.

A horrible sense of wrongness assailed her, gnawing at her resolution.

Almost a year ago Lia had believed that giving up her baby was the best thing she could do for him, her mind fogged by grief after Rico's death, and by the pressure that Zandro had unfairly put on her when she didn't have the strength to fight it. Surely taking Nicky back was only redressing a bad decision made under duress.

She tried to recapture the sense of righteousness and natural justice that had led her here, to overcome a mounting uncertainty.

Another rap on the door sent her to open it, expecting Mrs Walker again.

Zandro stood there, looking dark and intimidating, saying abruptly, 'I want to talk to you. Let me in.'

She hesitated, then stepped back.

He closed the door and she couldn't help a slight apprehension widening her eyes.

'It's all right,' he said impatiently, glancing over her with deliberate indifference that was a subtle insult. 'I have no designs on your body, Lia. I just don't want to be overheard.'

Annoyingly, her cheeks stung. 'You had something to say to me?'

'Yes. I'd appreciate it if you didn't start a quarrel in front of my mother. It upsets her. If you have any…criticism of my handling of my duties to Nicky— or anything else—bring it to me in private.'

'It takes two to make a quarrel.' She wasn't going to shoulder all the blame. 'You were the one making accusations. Am I supposed to take them lying down?'

His eyes darkened still further, then a muscle tightened subtly in his cheek, his mouth twitching as though he were biting back laughter. She saw his gaze shift to the big bed behind her, stop there, and something shivered in the air between them. Something that shocked and thrilled her at the same time.

At least a metre of space separated them, yet she could have sworn she felt heat emanating from his body, and she became acutely aware of how tall he was, how broad his shoulders were despite the leanness of his hips and the length of his powerful legs, yet he seemed perfectly proportioned. His collar was open, displaying a tantalising glimpse of light tan skin, and his mouth was an intriguing blend of firmness and softness, the masculine shape of it well defined. When after a heartbeat or two his eyes returned to her they appeared fathomless, as if a woman could drown in the unknowable depths of them.

Then he blinked and the strange moment passed, leaving her dazed, disoriented. 'No,' he said, and it was seconds before she realised he was answering her challenge. 'I admit I was at fault. In future perhaps we can both take more care.'

'I will if you will.' Flippancy was perhaps the way to dispel the lingering atmosphere that was making her feel heated and almost suffocated. Put that down to his size, which made the large room apparently shrink, and the fact that he was standing before the door, leaving her no way to get out.

But this was her room, even though she was a guest in the house. Standing her ground, she said, 'If that's all…?'

He looked as if it wasn't, as if there was more he wanted to say. The piercing speculation in his eyes made her feel he could read her mind, or at least was making uncomfortably accurate guesses at what was going on inside it. But he turned and opened the door, leaving without another word.

She spent some more time with Barbara and Nicky when the baby woke again. Feeling that the nanny might find her continued presence intrusive, after a while she left them and decided to walk on the beach.

It wasn't until the gates slid apart at her approach that she realised once they'd locked behind her she wouldn't be able to open them again. She didn't know the combination for the keypad, so would have to use the microphone in one of the gateposts and summon someone to let her in.

She hesitated, and heard footsteps behind her. Turning, she saw Zandro striding towards her along the driveway.

He wore sandals and swim briefs, a towel slung about his neck. And looked nothing short of magnificent. A man who had everything—good looks, a superb physique and the self-confidence that went with them. Even money.

He must have his pick of women eager to share his wealth, his life, yet he hadn't married, had no children of his own. Only his brother's child, who he was determined not to relinquish.

'Waiting for someone?' he inquired as he came closer, frowning at the open gateway.

'No.'

'Then don't stand there inviting all and sundry in.'

'I was going to the beach.'

His hard stare didn't waver. 'Come on then,' he said, and placed a hand on her waist, walking her out to the pavement as the gates closed behind them. 'Were you afraid of getting trapped in the gates?' he asked, pausing to check for traffic. 'If anything's in the way they won't close. It's quite safe.'

'I'd just realised,' she said as they began to cross the road, 'I don't know the combination to get back in.'

He didn't reply until they had gained the grass on the other side and he'd dropped his hand from her waist. 'If you press the button someone will open the gates from inside the house. You don't have to speak— there's a video camera as well as the microphone. It isn't necessary for you to have the code.'

She stopped, forcing him to halt and look at her. 'What you mean is that you don't trust me.'

'The fewer people who know it,' he said, 'the less likelihood of the code getting into the hands of burglars or…undesirables.'

'I'm not in the habit of consorting with burglars and undesirables!'

He gave a short, scornful laugh. 'As I recall, you and Rico had some very strange friends.'

'They might have been strange by your standards—'

'Potheads and worse! Dragging my brother into the gutter.' A rare flash of heat showed in his eyes, his voice.

'Rico wasn't in any gutter!'

'He was headed that way—and so were you.'

'No!'

Zandro's mouth tightened. 'The first step to beating an addiction is to admit to it.'

A sliver of uncertainty made her hesitate. 'I told you, I was never an addict. There was…a problem for a while with pills—tranquillisers, sleeping pills. Prescription drugs. I don't suppose you realise how easy it can be to become dependent on them.' She wouldn't mention the suicide attempt—that would give him ammunition if it ever came to a custody battle. But the memory renewed her antagonism. Zandro was at least partly to blame for that.

He was looking at her disbelievingly. 'When I found you and Rico in that seedy little flat the place reeked of marijuana.'

Oh, hell. Denying it was useless—he obviously had no doubt of what he'd smelled. She tried for nonchalance, shrugging a shoulder. 'Lots of people smoke socially. It…we'd had a party.'

He'd caught them at their worst, the morning after the night before, literally. Bodies all over the admittedly cramped apartment, sleeping off the effects. Nobody had cleaned up yet. After hauling Rico out of bed, ignoring Lia's shriek of protest, Zandro had ruthlessly shaken everyone else awake and dispatched them to the street, before fixing Rico with a condemning gaze and demanding to know what the hell he thought he was doing, and when he was going to straighten himself out and come home where he belonged.

'Are you saying,' he asked now with patent disbelief, 'you and Rico didn't…partake?'

Uncomfortable, she muttered, 'Maybe. Now and then. It's not like heroin or something.' She wasn't even sure what the current drug of fashion was among those in the scene. More strongly she added, 'Anyway, I don't even take aspirin if I can help it…now.'

His keen stare was still sceptical. 'You can swear to that, hand on heart?'

'Yes!' she said fervently. 'I have a baby to think of.'

'You certainly weren't doing much of that when I

found you in that damp, flea-ridden hole you were hiding in after Rico died.'

She said quietly, 'It wasn't a perfect environment for a child. If I hadn't realised that, do you think I'd have let you take him from me?'

'I didn't take him! I brought both of you back to Rico's home. You could have stayed if…'

Several teenagers on bicycles swerved off the road nearby and whooshed past, dividing around them. Zandro reached out to pull her closer as one of the bikes almost brushed against her. 'Watch where you're going!' he snapped at the cyclist. Although the manoeuvre had probably been quite deliberate, a bit of showing off.

The boy ignored him and pedalled off with his companions towards the beach, all of them whooping as their wheels went up a small rise and dropped to the sand.

Zandro scowled after them, then loosened his hold. 'Are you all right?'

'He didn't touch me.' Zandro had though, and even after he'd dropped his hand she could feel the imprint of his fingers on her flesh, had to stop herself from looking down to see if he'd left his mark on her again. Which was ridiculous. His clasp had been firm but not rough.

He cast her a seemingly baffled look, then said abruptly, 'I'm going for a swim.'

Swinging away from her, he strode across the grass to the beach and the water.

More slowly she followed to the gleaming white sand. Zandro's towel lay a few metres away. He was already waist deep in the water, and as she paused he plunged into an oncoming white-frilled wave.

It was a minute or so before she saw his black head emerge at the other side of the breaker, and his arms propelled him into a fast crawl.

After slipping off her flat canvas shoes she crossed the sand beyond the tide line and began to walk along the firmer part, parallel with the sea, in the opposite direction from the young cyclists who were now riding up to the grass and then down onto the sand, sometimes floundering and having to pick themselves up while their mates jeered and yahooed.

The beach was long and wide and remarkably empty. In the holiday season, she supposed, it would be filled.

She picked up a broken shell and tossed it aside, stopped to admire a lacy fragment of pink seaweed, lifted a bit of driftwood with a toe and hastily drew away from the hopping insects she'd disturbed.

Having walked a long way before turning back, she saw that Zandro had finished his swim and was sitting on his towel, knees drawn up. When she drew near he shaded his eyes with a hand, watching her.

It made her self-conscious, knowing the whippy breeze that had sprung up was blowing her hair about so that she had to finger strands away from her eyes, and moulding her dress against her body, the skirt sometimes catching between her thighs.

As she came close Zandro stood up, wrapping the towel about his taut waist. 'Had enough?' he queried.

'Yes. Were you waiting for me? There was no need.'

He glanced to where the boys had now left their bicycles lying on the sand and were sitting about smoking, although they looked too young to have bought cigarettes legally—supposing Australian law was similar to that back home. He said, 'I wouldn't leave you on the beach alone while they're here.'

'They're only kids.'

'Maybe, but I'm taking no chances.'

She halted on the grass to put on her shoes again, and he said, 'Going barefoot isn't always safe. There are stinging jellyfish in summer. And there's the chance of a stonefish hiding in the sand below the tide line.'

In New Zealand she and Nicky would be able to walk freely in the sand. Admittedly jellyfish weren't uncommon, and even sharks occasionally sent swimmers from the water, but they seldom troubled them unduly. And the killer stonefish were unknown.

After crossing the road at Zandro's side she wondered if he deliberately blocked her view while he keyed in the code to open the gates.

Probably. She tried to be amused, but his distrust rankled. A pinprick among other pinpricks that she'd suffered since entering the Brunellesci household.

She would have to put up with them for Nicky's sake.

Back at the house she went to her bathroom to wash sand from her feet and comb the tangles out of her hair. The walk had been refreshing and she'd relished the cool breeze that should have cleared her mind, but if anything she was more confused than before.

When Barbara collected Nicky before dinner she asked if he had a kiss for his mummy, and he presented his cheek, this time not drawing away. His skin was petal-like, and he smelled sweet and clean.

At dinner Domenico was stiffly polite, actually asking if she had enjoyed the park that morning.

'Yes,' she said. 'I'm sorry you weren't there.'

He gave her a piercing look that reminded her of his elder son, his whitening brows drawing together. 'I had other things to attend to,' he said. Then, rather grudgingly, with a glance at his wife, 'Perhaps tomorrow.'

Mrs Brunellesci was giving him an approving smile now. Obviously she knew the way to the old man's heart—if he had one.

Supposing the senior Brunellescis could be brought round to letting their grandchild go, surely they would persuade Zandro to agree. Domenico was no longer young, but he was male, and towards Barbara he acted as many elderly gentlemen did to women—with a courteous appreciation of her femininity. Despite his forbidding demeanour, maybe he was still susceptible to an attractive woman.

Anything that might help…

A smile might be a good idea. 'I'll look forward to it. I'm sure Nicky missed you.'

He looked startled, perhaps a little suspicious. Was she laying it on too thick? Zandro too was apparently sceptical, his eyes fixed on her with an inimical glint in them.

Possessed by a flash of mischief and a kind of reckless optimism, she smiled at him too—a deliberately dazzling smile.

The effect was not exactly what she'd hoped for. His eyes narrowed and his face took on a stiff, uncompromising expression.

Oh well, can't win 'em all. She looked away from him and concentrated on her food.

Next day when she and Barbara took Nicky to the park Domenico joined them. The old man watched her pushing the baby on the swing, catching him at the bottom of the slide, and helping Barbara teach him to build a sandcastle while he chatted away in baby language mixed with an occasional recognisable word.

A faint smile now and then relaxed Domenico's stern demeanour. On the way back to the house she fell into step beside him. 'Thank you,' she said quietly, 'for making sure Nicky was well cared for.'

A hint of surprise crossed his features. 'He's my grandson.'

'I thought you might not want to recognise him since he was…born outside of marriage.'

Disapproval creased the old man's brow. 'He has my son's blood. And mine.'

'But if you should have legitimate grandchildren—'

Domenico's stick thumped on the ground, his eyes flashing beneath the heavy brows as he turned to fully face her. 'You think we will repudiate Rico's child?'

'Zandro is the elder—'

'When Zandro marries,' the old man said, 'he will adopt Nicky. He has said so.'

CHAPTER FIVE

HER mouth fell open. Then she closed it, swallowing on a mixture of emotions—outrage, fear, shock. 'He can't do that!' Could he? Surely not. 'He…he'd have to have Nicky's mother's permission.' Quickly she added, 'And I'll never give it!'

Her raised voice had caught Barbara's attention, and Nicky's. He was looking at them, his eyes wide, the expression on his round face uncertain. She smiled distractedly to reassure him, and was rewarded by an answering grin showing a few little white teeth.

Biting her lip, she stalked beside Domenico the rest of the way to the house without speaking, her mind building up a bonfire of panicked anger.

It simmered for the remainder of the day, and although Domenico joined her and Mrs Brunellesci for lunch, and his manner even seemed to have thawed slightly, she found it difficult to maintain a polite conversation about trivialities.

Spending time afterwards with Nicky should have helped her relax, but as she solemnly accepted a thoroughly dead flower that had fallen on the lawn from one of the trees, and followed Barbara's example in naming things for him to try to repeat, inwardly she grew more tense. In the end she retreated to her room, lay on her bed and practised some relaxation exercises.

They didn't help much. Her mind was going around in circles, darting into corners and out again like a small caged animal. Closing her eyes didn't help, either. She saw Domenico's flashing eyes, Nicky's vulnerable innocence. And Zandro's unyielding determination. Felt again a limp, cold hand held in her reassuring fingers, saw pleading green eyes reflecting back like a mirror the same anguished love and sorrow that she knew were in hers. Heard the echo of her own voice, thick with tears. 'I give you my solemn promise… Yes, yes, of course I'll bring him up just as you want. I won't let them ruin your son's life, too.'

When she heard Zandro's car drive into the garage she got up, glimpsed a pale face and dishevelled hair in the dressing table mirror, and paused to quickly use a comb and apply a defensive swipe of lipstick before going downstairs. Waylaying him looking as though she'd just got out of bed would do nothing for her confidence.

Zandro didn't appear, and after spending a few minutes hanging about in the deserted hallway she left the house by a rear door where there was no numbered security lock, and mooched about the back garden for a while, not wanting to hunt him down or ask someone where he could be found. He'd probably headed straight to his room to change, and she'd missed hearing him somehow.

Maybe he would go for a swim again. Then she could catch him when he came out of the water. She turned towards the front of the house and made for the beach.

Zandro wasn't in sight, even when she shaded her eyes and gazed out to sea. A couple of surfboarders rode the waves, and a lone windsurfer dipped and swayed in the distance, but she saw no swimmers.

Spurts of sand blew about in the breeze, and high dark clouds drifted across the sky, intermittently obscuring the sun. Locals would perhaps find it too cool for swimming. Rubbing goose flesh on her arms, she wished she'd brought a light sweater to put over the sleeveless tank top she wore with her cotton skirt. It wasn't summer yet, and although warmer than Auckland when she'd left there, Queensland could still turn on a slight chill.

The grassy bank curved about the sand to form a small, sheltered hollow that she huddled into, her arms resting on raised knees. She'd always found the sea soothing to her soul back home, watching the endless waves roll in and unfold onto the shore before drawing back to gather strength from the depths of the ocean and hurl themselves again at the land, inch by inch wearing away at it until rock turned to grains of sand.

Water was more powerful than it seemed. And like rock, maybe Zandro could be worn down. Only she didn't have aeons to do it in.

Deathbed promises were a sacred trust. She set her chin, summoned all her courage and steadfastness against a wavering conviction.

Surely Rico had known his own family and what they were capable of. She had been so clear in her mind that she had to remove Nicky before the Brunellescis wrecked his life as they had wrecked his father's.

And not only Rico's. Overcome with a wave of sorrow, she dropped her head onto her folded arms, hot tears stinging her eyes.

She let them fall silently. There was no one to see, no one to care, and she'd been fighting this ever since she arrived. Since some time before that. Keeping her mind—once she'd managed to focus it properly and push the first tearing grief into the background—on what must be done to fulfil her solemn vow.

The world fell away in a rush of memories—happy ones laced with bitterness, sadness and anger at the waste of young life, the tragedy of a fatherless, motherless child, the blind intransigence of one family.

When the tears finally stopped a long time later she remained as she was, feeling drained, lifeless, until she jerked up her head in startled response to Zandro's single sharp, *'Lia?'*

She shouldn't have looked at him, she realised immediately. Her eyes felt gritty, the lids swollen and hot. She glimpsed his body—wet swim briefs clinging to lean hips, his chest gleaming with salt water—before she looked away, ducking her head.

Too late. He dropped to one knee, the thick white towel he held falling in a heap on the sand. His big hand grasped her chin, lifting her face. 'You're crying.' He seemed taken aback.

'I'm not!' She jerked from his hold, staring stubbornly, unblinking, at the sea behind him.

His thumb brushed away a trail of salt moisture that hadn't quite dried on her cheek. 'You have been.'

She didn't bother to deny it this time.

'For Rico?' he asked, as if he found it hard to believe.

Throwing him a scornful glance, she said, 'You don't think I could have loved your brother? He was very loveable.'

She knew he hadn't missed the implied, *Not like you.* Her anger had returned, reinforced by the humiliating fact that he'd found her in tears, showing a weakness she'd determined not to let him see.

'I know that,' he said harshly, and she recognised pain as well as anger in the sudden tightness of his mouth, even in his eyes.

However imperfectly and misguidedly, he must have loved his brother. He'd cared enough to pursue him to Sydney and try to set him on what the family had seen as the right path.

'You just didn't understand him,' she said.

As an olive branch it failed disastrously. Zandro's head snapped upwards and he looked at her with hostility. 'And you think you did?'

Hotly, she said, 'Couldn't you see that you were driving him further away with your demands on him—you and your father? That he wasn't suited to a business life?'

'He wasn't suited to any kind of life as an adult,' Zandro snapped. 'My mother spoiled him and my father let her do it. Rico never learned to take responsibility—for himself or anyone else. It's probably just as well for Nicky that his father isn't around anymore.'

Her gasp of protest made him clamp his mouth shut. 'How can you say that,' she cried, 'about your own *brother?* Are you *glad* he's dead?' This was surely his true self, the one Rico had described. She couldn't let herself be fooled by his other, more human face.

Zandro's cheekbones whitened. Roughly he said, 'Of course not. But his son is better off now than he would have been if Rico had continued on the path where he was headed.'

'Money isn't everything.'

Zandro made an impatient gesture. 'I'm not talking about money. I know there are other things more important for a child.'

'Like his mother!' The reminder of what he'd done helped to whip her anger into fury.

That seemed to pull him up. 'It depends,' he said

slowly, looking at her in a probing, almost puzzled way, 'on what sort of mother she is.'

'One who loved—*loves* him!' she said tensely. 'Who even gave him up to *you* when she thought it was the only way to ensure a decent future for him. Who would have torn out her heart for him. Who *did.*'

She thought she'd shaken him a bit. He hadn't moved, and she realised how close he was, so she could see the slight difference in the inky colour of his eyes where the pupils merged into the irises. Then he blinked, his lashes long and thick and very black, momentarily hiding his eyes before he gave her another searching look. 'That wasn't how you struck me at the time.'

'You're not very observant, are you?' she suggested.

He tilted his head as if considering, remembering, his eyes still studying her face.

Uneasy, she dropped her arms from her knees and shifted her legs to one side, recalling that she'd wanted to confront him. Baldly, aggressively, she said, 'Your father said you intend to adopt Nicky.'

He blinked again, and his bare shoulders moved. 'Supposing I marry. It would safeguard him if I had other children. Give him equal rights.'

'To your fortune?' she queried with scorn.

Zandro shrugged. 'That, and all that being part of a family implies.'

'Like being forced into the family firm?'

A frown appeared between the black brows. Sounding exasperated, he argued, 'No one will force him into anything. He'll certainly be given the chance to help run the business if that's what he wants.'

'That's not how it was with Rico.'

The frown deepened. 'Whatever Rico wanted, he

got. He *needed* discipline, but that was the one thing he *wasn't* given. It will be different with Nicky.'

Going cold, she said, 'You mean you'll beat him into submission?' And fiercely, 'Over my dead body!'

The words reminded her of how this situation had come about in the first place. Hatefully, tears threatened again, and she began to struggle to her feet. She had to get away from here, from Zandro. Either to pull herself together or indulge her renewed grief in private.

The yielding sand impeded her rising, and Zandro reached out and stayed her, bringing her to her knees in front of him, his hands on her arms, his own knees touching hers. 'Hang on a minute,' he said.

'Let me go!' He smelled of the sea water drying on his skin. His hair was sleeked back, making his lean features appear stone-hewed, and she could see the rise and fall of his broad brown chest with his breathing. There was an overpowering masculinity about him that aroused conflicting feelings—a stirring of desire that shocked her, followed by a frightened anger with both herself and him, then appalled shame, and panic.

She pushed against the immovable, warm wall of his chest with closed fists, and had no effect. Rage overwhelming everything else, she glared into his grimly determined face and alert, fiercely questioning eyes, and tried to hit him, but he was too quick. A hand caught her wrist like an iron bracelet, then despite her brief, desperate resistance, he captured both wrists and wrestled her to her back, one of his legs bent across hers, pinning her to the sand.

Pure terror knifed through her for an instant. He was so strong, so big, and he looked as angry as she, his eyes glittering under narrowed lids, his face taut, relentless. When he spoke his teeth showed, white and dangerous. 'I've never laid a finger on Nicky,' he said in a voice equally dangerous. 'And I never will. There are other ways of instilling discipline in a child. I don't believe in physical coercion. Does that satisfy you?'

'Obviously your fine principles don't extend to women!' she flung at him, still held in that iron grip. Fury overcame her fear, her eyes hotly accusing.

She was gratified to see a shadow of stunned guilt cross his face, as if he hadn't realised what he was doing. He released her, sat back on his haunches and ran a hand through his damp hair. 'I lost my temper,' he admitted, his voice grating.

'And I'm supposed to believe you'll never do the same with Nicky?' Sitting up, she sent him a challenging stare.

'I didn't hurt you, did I?' he countered. 'You were the one who tried to hit me.'

'Self-defence! You had no right to grab me.'

His inclined head seemed to reluctantly acknowledge the point. 'I don't appreciate being portrayed as a child abuser.' His expression changing again, his gaze knife-like. 'Did you imagine I was going to attack you?'

She hadn't known what was in his mind, only that she'd been briefly scared witless. 'It's a public place,' she said, loathe to allow him the satisfaction of knowing he could do that to her.

'And you think someone would have rescued you?' he scorned. 'With that naive attitude you're inviting trouble.'

'Do *you* think you have a God-given right to physically restrain a woman who tries to walk away from you?'

'No.' He clipped out the single word. 'It's never been necessary before.'

For an instant she was breathless at his hubris. 'Lucky you! I suppose they fall at your feet of their own accord.' She began to rise again. '*Now* do you mind if I go?'

He stood up too as she turned from him, stopping her this time with his voice alone, compelling and inflexible. 'That isn't what I meant. No woman ever threw a charge like that at me without giving me a chance to refute it. I wasn't about to let you do that.'

She'd been so intent on regaining her equilibrium, escaping his disturbing presence, she'd almost forgotten what had started the contretemps. 'It's immaterial anyway,' she said recklessly, 'because you're not going to adopt Nicky.' Or even remain his guardian for much longer, she devoutly hoped. 'I will *never* sign a consent for that.'

She left him standing, climbed the shallow bank and was halfway across the park before he caught up with her. He'd slung the towel about his neck and she was conscious of him easily keeping pace with her. It distracted her so that she almost stepped into the road without thinking. He grabbed at her arm and hauled her back as a car came sweeping along in front of them, travelling at a speed way over the limit.

She shook his hand away, throwing him a hostile stare, and surprising a grim amusement in his eyes. The street was empty, but she looked carefully this time before walking across to the gateway.

Zandro opened it, and joined her again on the driveway. 'We both have to consider Nicky's welfare above everything else, Lia,' he said.

'I am!'

'Are you sure?' They were approaching the house, and when she looked at him she saw he was staring up at its muted gold magnificence. 'Do you still want to take him from a home where he's happy and secure?'

'He's just a baby. He'll forget.' Smothering her recent qualms with a confident tone.

His jaw tautened. 'Is that what you want for him? That he'll forget his father's family? His grandparents who took him in almost from birth, cared for him—who love him?'

She could see no other way. And yet...

He had some right on his side, she knew, sickeningly. She could lie—again—and say that Rico's family would be welcome to keep in touch, see Nicky if they cared to make the journey to New Zealand. But she was unable to bring herself to offer the specious reassurance.

'Think about what you'd be doing to him,' Zandro urged.

They reached the wide steps and he placed a light hand on her arm. It must be automatic with him, something he did for any female, a token courtesy he was scarcely even aware of. But she could feel that touch affect every part of her body, making her warm and weak-kneed.

She supposed some men carried a sexual charge that no woman could totally ignore, and he was one of them. Nothing to do with love, or even liking. Long before meeting him she had disliked Zandro Brunellesci. Rico had apparently been fond of him despite his awe of his big brother, but Lia had never understood why. From all Rico had told her Zandro had sounded callous and money-grubbing, with more pride than was good for anyone, rigidly moralistic and unbearably arrogant.

And his treatment of her both before and after Rico's

death had only reinforced that impression. Except, perhaps, when he had persuaded her to give up her son. Then he'd used a mixture of persuasion and coercion. Did he hope to do so again?

Zandro punched in more numbers at the front door and turned to usher her into the hallway. 'Why are you looking at me like that?' he queried, his brows lifting.

He was smart, this man. He knew what buttons to push. Gates, doors—people. For him there was little difference. She must remember that.

She shrugged. 'I don't know what you mean.'

'I think you do.'

Making to pass him, she was stopped by his hand on her arm. Her breast brushed across his bare chest, and she flinched away, her back coming up against the doorjamb.

He let her go, but something held her still, perhaps the strange look in his eyes, as though he'd never really looked at her before and now saw something he hadn't expected.

The air in the few inches between them seemed thick with invisible tension. 'What do you want, Lia?' he asked, an odd question for this moment. His voice was pitched low—a velvet seduction.

She blinked, trying to break a peculiar spell that seemed to hold her in thrall. 'You know what I want. Nicky.' Defiantly she added, 'My son.'

The silence stretched, and his eyes didn't waver from hers. She stared back at him, willing him to give in, to make it easy for her, to let her go—and take his brother's baby with her.

'No.' The word was flat, definite.

She'd known, of course, that his answer would be the same as before. But in these last few seconds something had altered subtly, some new factor entering the equation. He'd seen something in her eyes, and his own had changed, darkened still further, with a deep glow in them.

'I'll try to work something out,' he said.

A concession? Or a sop—an empty half-promise? 'Visiting rights?' she queried. 'I told you, that's not enough.'

He moved then, irritably, thrusting his hands into his pockets, shifting away from the door, allowing her to escape the invisible net that had briefly entrapped them. She took a gulp of air and he said, 'Give me time, Lia. The situation's too complicated to resolve in a couple of days.'

Barbara had the weekend off. On Saturday Nicky joined the family for breakfast, his high chair carried into the conservatory by Zandro.

Mrs Brunellesci ensconced the boy into it as Zandro pulled out chairs for the two women, commenting, 'You look very…sunny this morning, Lia.' His lightning glance passed over the sleeveless cotton dress patterned with large sunflowers. She said, 'I thought Nicky would like it.'

A faint smile curved Zandro's lips as he took a chair near Nicky. 'It suits you.'

He could be charming when he tried. Reminding herself he almost certainly had an ulterior motive, she said stiffly, 'I'd like to feed him if that's all right.'

Zandro's lips curved further, as though her deliberate deflection of the compliment amused him. 'Of course,' he said. 'But he's very independent.'

That was true, and she soon discovered why having Nicky at the dining table wasn't a daily occurrence.

After the meal she wiped up some of the mess, and was carrying the baby up the stairs to clean and change him when Zandro came down wearing tennis shorts and carrying a racquet.

He stood back against the wall to let her pass, although the stairs were wide enough for her to have done so without that courtesy.

'Don't leave the house until I come back,' he said.

'I won't abscond with him,' she retorted. 'I suppose you've directed your minions to stop me if I try.'

He didn't answer, but she was sure she could feel his gaze following her.

Once the baby was clean and fresh she and Nicky spent the morning with his grandmother in the garden, and even Domenico joined them for a while, perusing the weekend newspaper.

At lunchtime when they went inside Zandro came to the table in light trousers and a casual shirt, his hair damp from a shower and combed back, throwing into relief his strong profile with its classical imperious nose and inflexible chin.

His good looks were striking—even Rico had surely never equalled his brother. In every way he must have grown up in Zandro's shadow—younger, less talented, less strong and much less sure of himself and his place in the world. As the firstborn son, Zandro had no comparable insecurities—and there was surely not enough room for two such powerful personalities in one family, one business. No wonder Rico had to escape, to find his own life away from his stronger, smarter, more self-confident brother, who so closely resembled their father. A father who, despite their estrangement, Rico had named his son for.

Zandro turned from speaking to Domenico, his decisive brows lifting a little in silent inquiry. 'Lia?'

'Nothing.' He'd caught her watching him. A disconcerting, knowing glint entered his eyes before she averted hers, forking a slice of salami onto her plate. Lunch was cold meats, cheese, bread and salad, with a bowl of fresh fruit on the table. Mrs Walker had set everything out and left them to help themselves.

When Nicky decisively refused any more offers of food and became restless, she pushed back her chair to stand and offer her arms before anyone else could forestall her.

'He'll be all right crawling round the floor,' Zandro said. 'Finish your meal, Lia.'

'I've finished, and I'd like some time alone with him.'

Their eyes clashed, and she held the authoritative gaze defiantly. Damned if she was going to ask for Zandro's permission. 'We'll be in his room.'

She turned and left, half expecting another command for her to stay, but it didn't come.

Thirty minutes later she was reading a picture book aloud to Nicky while he sat on her lap in a tub chair when Zandro entered through the open door.

She stopped reading and Nicky made a sound of protest, slapping his hand onto the book and fixing her with a stern, round-eyed stare.

'Go on, Lia,' Zandro said, leaning against the doorjamb and sliding his hands into his trouser pockets, apparently content to wait.

Feeling self-conscious, she finished the rest of the book and closed it. Nicky wriggled down and made for the doorway, to be scooped up by Zandro and cradled in his arms.

'Dee, dio,' the little boy crooned, patting a lean male cheek.

'*Zio,*' Zandro confirmed. 'Uncle. Ready to go for a drive, young man?'

He wanted to take Nicky away? Standing up, she protested, 'I've only had half an hour with him.'

'You can come along,' Zandro said indifferently.

'Oh, thank you!' Quite unable to keep the sarcasm from her voice.

'It's a regular arrangement. An elderly friend of my mother's is crippled by arthritis and in a nursing home. She has no children and she looks forward to these visits. Mamma has been taking Nicky with her once a month since he was a babe in arms. The residents make a fuss of him, and he thoroughly enjoys it. Afterwards we usually take him somewhere special—a new play-ground or to visit friends with children. It allows me to spend time with him.'

She couldn't object to that. 'Barbara didn't say...'

'Barbara doesn't need to know what happens on her days off. She will have packed a bag for him, though. Here, you take Nicky and I'll carry the bag.'

He seemed to take it for granted she was coming, and she carried the baby downstairs and sat in the back beside him after Zandro strapped Nicky into his car seat.

At the nursing home Mrs Brunellesci's friend waited in the big lounge where several elderly people sat read-ing, doing handiwork or dozing in their chairs. She welcomed Nicky with a huge smile and open arms, and after a slight initial hesitation he seemed happy to sit on her knee and play with the half-dozen strings of beads she wore about her neck.

'This is Lia,' Mrs Brunellesci introduced her while

Zandro parked the baby bag on the floor by the other woman's chair. Her friend offered a smile, a clawlike hand and a heavily accented greeting, then made some remark in Italian that Mrs Brunellesci replied to in the same language.

Zandro said quietly, 'Mrs Pisano's English is not good. Perhaps we could walk in the garden, Lia, while the ladies talk.'

He steered her outside to an extensive lawn with brightly coloured flowerbeds, and seats set under shady trees. One of the seats was occupied by an elderly man and a younger woman, while two children chased each other about nearby, squealing and giggling.

An archway covered in purpling bougainvillaea led to a paved patio surrounded by a clipped hedge. In the centre a small fountain splashed into a round pool where several goldfish darted about.

'Shall we sit down?' Zandro suggested. 'In the shade?' The hedge shadowed one side of the patio, and he guided her to a seat there, leaving at least a foot of space between them as he leaned back to contemplate the fountain, his arms folded and long legs stretched out before him. For some time neither of them spoke.

The sound of the water, and the sun sparkling on the falling droplets, was hypnotic, the faint rustling of leaves in the nearby trees soothing, and although at first she sat stiffly, within minutes the tension in her body eased.

As if he'd been waiting for that, Zandro stirred, angling his body slightly to lean a forearm on the back of the seat and study her face before he spoke. 'Barbara tells me you're good with Nicky.'

She cast him a fleeting glance, then looked back at the fountain. 'You asked her to report to you?'

His gaze didn't waver; she could feel it. 'I'm responsible for your child, Lia, whether you like it or not.'

She looked at him then, rebellion in her face. 'I won't let you and your father do to him what you did to Rico.'

His eyes flashed with temper. 'We did nothing to harm Rico! What happened to him was his own doing.' He paused as she averted her head, her lips tight. He gripped her arms and made her face him again, both his hands holding her below the short sleeves of her dress. 'Whatever he felt, and however many mistakes my parents made—as all parents do—they loved him and wanted him to be happy. And so did I.'

'He *was* happy in Sydney, away from the pressures you and your parents put on him! And with someone he loved—who loved him! Why didn't you just leave him alone?'

'How could I?' Zandro demanded roughly. 'Leave him to sink further into the drug culture you'd dragged him into, and wreck his life completely?'

Shock widened her eyes and for an instant held her speechless. Then she tried to wrench herself from him. 'I…I *didn't!*' Remembering she'd admitted to smoking marijuana occasionally, she said, 'He…we weren't doing hard drugs. I've never been into that and—' with spurious confidence '—neither was Rico.'

Zandro's eyes narrowed. 'You're an accomplished liar.'

Not by choice, not usually. She shook her head, ashamed that she was unable to deny it, or to excuse herself without giving away far too much. 'No.' But it was a faint protest, unconvincing. Rallying, she tried again. 'It's the truth.' As far as she knew it.

After a moment he said, 'Maybe I'm blaming you unfairly—he made his own choices—but I saw the marks on his arms, and you must have known he was injecting.'

'Marks?' she echoed, dread forming a growing lump in her chest. 'You...you were mistaken.'

'You're in denial,' he said flatly. 'Why? Are you still taking stuff yourself?' He released one arm, but only to take her other wrist and turn it so he could inspect her inner elbow.

His fingers were digging into her skin; he didn't know his own strength—or didn't care. But she was too distressed to complain.

His hold relaxed and she managed to pull herself away, standing up and backing from him until stopped by the edge of the fountain. Fine cool droplets dampened her shoulders but she ignored them, already feeling her blood running cold in her veins. Her voice thin, she said, 'You're making this up.'

He stood then too. 'Why the hell would I make up something like that about my own brother?'

Her head was whirling. He sounded so positive— could he possibly *know* this? Had she been naive, blinded by love and sympathy? Weakly she suggested, 'Maybe you're jealous.' He'd told her his mother doted on Rico, that the younger brother had been spoiled by both their parents.

The effect of her wild speculation was extraordinary. Zandro's cheeks darkened, and for once he seemed at a loss, looking almost guilty, thick lashes momentarily hiding his eyes before a scowl drew his brows inward and his mouth became a thin line. 'Jealous?' He cast a deliberately insulting look over her, an explicit mental stripping that she'd never before been subjected to, making her feel both physically and emotionally exposed.

She shivered as though he had truly removed every stitch of clothing, of protection, from her body, leaving her naked. Her whole being shrank from the crudely sexist scrutiny, the total lack of respect he quite knowingly displayed.

He gave a short, harsh laugh, reinforcing his open contempt. 'I've never had any reason to be jealous of my brother,' he stated. His face became impassive, so that she could almost have imagined that searing perusal. He made an impatient gesture. 'And certainly not now.'

Because Rico was dead. And Lia…

Snatching at a startling, appalling thought, she said, finding her voice, 'You think if you accuse Nicky's parents of drug abuse you'll have permanent custody! I'll take tests if necessary—they'll prove I'm not taking anything! *Nothing,*' she emphasised. 'Nada!'

'Perhaps that's true—now,' he said slowly. 'What about the past…and the future? I could get some of those so-called friends of yours from Sydney to tell a judge what they know about you.'

Her mouth went dry. 'Even if you found them they wouldn't…'

Zandro cut in as her voice trailed off uncertainly. 'I'll find them—I have the resources—and don't count on them. When I was searching for Rico, most of them would have sold their souls for the money to buy their next hit.'

He was so sure of his ground she had to believe he was telling the terrible truth. Accept what she'd refused to allow into her mind before.

The sun beating on her hair made her dizzy, so that

she swayed on her feet and closed her eyes to clear her head.

Suddenly Zandro's familiar masculine scent was in her nostrils, and a strong arm came about her. 'Are you ill?' he asked sharply.

She tried to pull away from him but he held her, an impersonal hold although her shoulder was pressed against his chest and she felt the masculine hardness of his body. He said, 'You'd better sit down again.'

'No.' She needed to get away from him, to think clearly, and it wasn't possible with him so close as he tried to urge her back to the seat. Pushing against him again, she dislodged his grip on her and put some space between them, unbalancing herself in the process so that she fell against the fountain, one hand slipping into cold water, before Zandro caught her, hauled her upright and into his arms.

Instinctively she clutched at him, and they stood breast to breast, thigh to thigh, a shock of purest physical sensation passing through her and making her lift her face to stare into dark eyes that stared back at her intently, purposefully, making her shiver—not with cold but with a fierce, breathtaking anticipation.

CHAPTER SIX

HER heart thudded. She seemed surrounded by Zandro's seductive aroma, his chin against her temple, her breasts pressed to the wall of his chest. He muttered something and she saw his eyes were black and cheekbones taut, his nostrils flaring subtly as he breathed sharply inward. For once he was less than in full control, his expression angry and tortured, as if he was conducting some kind of internal warfare.

Then his head blotted out the sun and involuntarily she closed her eyes again, just before his mouth descended on hers in a kiss that snatched her breath and sent the blood in her veins racing, hot and heavy. He gave her no chance of denial, his lips arrogantly parting hers, a purposeful hand on her chin, fingers forcing her mouth further open to an exploration that held both naked, violent desire and pent-up rage.

The world seemed to swirl about her, then she was plunged into a dark abyss of passion, a perilous enthrallment, imprisoned by his arms, his body, completely taken over by the kiss that allowed her no escape and no mercy.

When he finally dropped his arms she saw he looked nearly as dazed as she felt, and he had to catch her again, his hands on her elbows until she dragged herself away, staring into his face, that he was now ordering into an inscrutable mask.

This was impossible—dangerously so. She had to take control somehow. 'What the hell,' she whispered,

91

pushing a strand of hair from her forehead, 'was that all about?'

His mouth moved in a tight grimace that might have been meant for a smile. 'A man and a woman,' he said. 'An impulse.' He lifted a shoulder. 'Perhaps it was inevitable.'

She shook her head vehemently. 'Because...?' she managed to ask. Then caustically, 'You can't resist coming on to any woman within kissing distance?'

This time his smile was almost genuine, though it held a sting of derision, perhaps for himself rather than her. 'I'm more discriminating than that, Lia. And I didn't notice you objecting.'

'You didn't give me a chance!'

He silently raised his brows, and she bit her lip, aware that she hadn't protested or struggled, had been stunned by the unleashing of his dazzling sexuality into acquiescence if not reciprocation. Not dwelling on that, she said, 'We don't even like each other! You despise me!'

'This...thing that's been simmering between us ever since we met...again—' a hint of perplexity briefly entered his eyes '—doesn't have any connection to liking.'

'You've got that right!' She was still trying to regain her equilibrium.

'But if you've really kicked your drug habit,' he said grudgingly, 'I'd have to say I respect you for that.'

She blinked at him in surprise. 'You don't believe me. You made that clear.'

'Let's say I'm keeping an open mind.'

'Let's say,' she echoed, 'that you're capable of doing that.'

Unexpectedly he laughed. A real laugh, and when

he looked at her again his gaze was concentrated, as if he was trying to work out something. It was not the first time he'd studied her like that, and it made her jittery. 'Maybe,' he suggested, 'you might do the same. My parents aren't monsters, Lia. They could only do what seemed right at the time. No one's perfect—and certainly not me. But I swear to you I have always, and will always, do the best I can for Rico's son.'

'What you think is best may not be the right thing for him.'

'And you believe you could do better, just because you're his mother?'

Pushing away the sneaking thought that his scepticism might be justified, she retorted, 'A single man who's not even a father is hardly an ideal parent.'

'That's why I hired a nanny. And Nicky has his grandparents. You told me your mother and father were dead.'

'Yes, but—'

He held up his hands. 'Let's not get into this argument again. You hardly know Nicky yet.'

'And whose fault is that?' she shot at him.

His lips compressed, but he only said quite mildly, 'If you want to hold me responsible I accept that. Only I can't say I'm sorry. I could see no other way at the time.'

On the journey home past sparsely grassed farmland that seemed strangely empty, and sometimes alongside the sea, suspicion kicked in. In the middle of a quarrel, after openly showing his disdain for her, and for her supposed drug habit, Zandro had kissed her—with undeniable passion, but also with banked anger that he couldn't hide.

His self-control was absolute. Even if the kiss had been an impulse, there must have been a motive.

The man had more than his fair share of sexual charisma and knew how to exploit it. He'd pulled out all stops to obtain custody of his brother's child in the first place, but hadn't at that point been crass enough to imagine that a woman mourning her recently dead lover would succumb to sexual advances.

This was a new and disquieting strategy.

Momentarily it crossed her mind that she might possibly turn it to her own advantage—if Zandro was genuinely attracted to her, even against his own formidable will.

She tried to banish the idea, disgusted at herself, but found her mind returning to it after they arrived home and she'd gone upstairs to her bedroom. Feeling hot and sticky, she decided to shower and change before dinner.

Stepping under the spray, she shivered, although the water was warm. 'No,' she said aloud. Using sex to get what she wanted went against every principle she held. Besides, the idea was fraught with several kinds of horrendous risk.

Already she'd done battle with and compromised several ingrained principles, not least her honesty, and she was daily risking her reputation, possibly even her physical safety if Zandro ever discovered her deception. She'd do anything to rescue Nicky from a future of unhappiness and oppressive expectations. *Had* done things that normally would have appalled her. But surely there was an easier way than placing her own heart and soul in jeopardy.

On Sunday morning the whole family went to church. Nicky was happy to climb from one lap to another and sit quietly for a time, apparently enthralled by the candles, the singing, the movement, and even during the sermon was easily occupied with a picture book and Mrs Brunellesci's rosary beads.

Afterwards the house seemed full of people. Domenico had no other family in Australia, but Mrs Brunellesci's sister and her husband, and their two daughters who both had young families of their own, arrived for Sunday brunch.

'You remember Lia,' Zandro said, a hand on her waist as his cousins first stared at her in surprise, then kissed her on both cheeks, and their husbands followed. Children milled about, two little girls making a beeline for Nicky, who was happy to be picked up and made a fuss of, obviously quite at home with his extended family.

It was difficult to remember all the names, even more difficult to answer questions about life in New Zealand without giving herself away, tiptoeing around a minefield of fact and near-fiction. Especially since Zandro, even while talking to other people, seemed to be listening to her replies.

His nerve-racking interest in her was unremitting and concentrated, and she found it impossible to put yesterday's searing episode out of her mind. Even without looking at him she knew exactly where he was every moment of the day, as if he held some psychic thread that connected them and that she couldn't escape. It was disturbing and distracting, and she wasn't sure if it was something he did consciously or if the phenomenon was all in her own mind.

After the family left, late in the afternoon, the house became very quiet. Nicky was having an overdue nap, and Mrs Brunellesci had dozed off in an armchair. Domenico announced he was going for a walk, his stick tapping on the tiles as he left.

'You look tired, Lia,' Zandro remarked, watching her pick up toys that Nicky and his cousins had left on the floor and various chairs, and replace them in a plastic basket. She tried to ignore him, discount the fact that for the first time that day they were alone, and not give him any hint of her inner turmoil.

He stooped to fish a teddy bear from under an occasional table and add it to the collection.

'Your family en masse is rather…overwhelming.'

'Nicky loves them.'

A deliberate reminder, she knew. Nicky had certainly enjoyed playing with his cousins, and they'd been rather sweetly attentive to him.

She placed a board book in the basket and looked around for more toys. Zandro found a lone wooden block and handed it to her. 'I overheard you saying you have no family in New Zealand?'

Tears threatened, and she looked away. 'I have good friends.' But if she carried out her intentions she'd have to cut herself off from them, start afresh somewhere new. Her heart shrank, and she tried to bolster her faltering courage, setting her jaw and unconsciously tightening her hands on the basket.

Zandro said, 'Don't you have a sister?'

Her whole body went rigid and she almost stopped breathing. Not daring to look at him and barely moving her lips, she said, 'Not anymore.'

After a moment he queried quietly, 'She died?'

Her throat blocked, she nodded. It occurred to her she might have denied ever having a sister, but that would have felt like a further betrayal.

'I'm very sorry, Lia.' A pause. 'Recently?'

'Yes.' Only a matter of weeks, scarcely months. 'I don't want to talk about it.'

She looked down at the basket, picked a small stuffed toy up and then dropped it back. Casting about for more things to tidy up, she started to turn away, but Zandro reached out and firmly took the basket from her, placing it on a nearby table. He captured one of her hands, startling her. 'Relax,' he said, taking the other hand too, in a strong but gentle grip. 'I'm not your enemy, Lia.'

Only yesterday he had been, unequivocally so. Her nerves screamed caution. Was this simply a new tactic to get his way? Persuade her to give up the fight? Did he know that his touch scrambled her brain, made her body recall the devastating kiss yesterday and, despite the anger she'd sensed behind it, perfidiously yearn for more?

With an effort she pulled her hands away and clenched them at her sides. His expression cooled. He said, 'Have you thought about moving to Australia?'

'I can't do that!' She hoped he didn't hear the alarm in her tone. It would complicate things still further. Make her even more vulnerable.

'Can't?' He frowned. 'We need to find some kind of compromise. Surely you can see that?'

From his point of view she supposed it seemed logical. He couldn't know that compromise for her was impossible. Unless... 'Would you give Nicky up?' she asked. 'If I lived here?'

He was silent for long seconds. 'I can't promise that,' he said finally.

At least he was honest. She turned away from him,

impatiently pushing back her hair with both hands. Time she had it cut again.

Zandro evidently didn't make promises he couldn't keep. Her own promises troubled her. She'd made them in good faith, not knowing how difficult it would be to carry them out.

She sighed, and Zandro said, 'Why don't you rest for a while before dinner?'

Half-turning, she gave him a crooked little smile and shook her head. Her body might rest, away from his too-vibrant presence, but her mind would be in overdrive, twisting and turning, trying to find a way out of this mess. 'What are *you* going to do?' she asked distractedly, simply for something to say, an attempt at diverting herself from her thoughts.

'Swim.' He briefly turned his head to the window where the sea was just visible through the iron gates. Looking back at her, he said rather abruptly, 'You could come along if you like.'

Surprise stilled her. His eyes met hers in silent, perhaps even reluctant challenge, and a subtle vibration in the air quickened her breath and sent a shot of adrenaline through her veins. She was somehow convinced he hadn't meant to issue the invitation, was instantly regretting it, but Zandro would never back down. Maybe he was waiting for her to refuse, let him off the hook.

She should say no. She knew it. The sensible thing was to retreat from this disquieting and surely precarious shift in the balance of their relationship—if their interaction could even be called a relationship.

But inside her a strange, reckless curiosity stirred, a compelling need to know this man with his complex, contradictory psyche and his sizzling sexuality, to abandon caution and explore this new and rather frightening sensation. 'All right,' she heard herself say, her voice scarcely her own. 'I'll get changed.' After all, she rationalised, if she failed in her avowed undertaking it would be imperative to salvage whatever she could, and an understanding of Zandro Brunellesci would be absolutely necessary to mitigate the disaster.

'Put something on your feet,' he instructed.

This was mad, she told herself minutes later, catching a glimpse of herself in the mirror, long legs emerging from a skimpy swimsuit that clung to every contour of her body. Where the top dipped between her breasts it was more revealing than she remembered.

She slipped her feet into flat-heeled thong sandals, picked up a large towel and fastened it under her arms like a sarong before going downstairs, tempted to chicken out even now. But when she saw Zandro in the hallway, a towel slung about his neck, briefs low on his narrow hips, and his eyes watching her descent with a bold, intent stare, she knew it wasn't an option. She met his gaze steadily and refused to look away, keeping her expression neutral.

Silently he opened the door for her and they walked side by side down the drive and over to the park.

The water was cold when she plunged into the waves after Zandro and emerged gasping on the far side of a breaker. His sleek head broke through the surface seconds later, only a metre away. 'Okay?' he asked her.

'Yes.' She breast-stroked away from him, but he followed, staying not far off but never close enough to touch.

Once the first chill receded, the sea was exhilarating, cooler than the swimming pool that absorbed the sun's heat, and when they finally left it she felt fully alive, tingling all over, the salt water running down her skin.

She rubbed her towel over her hair while Zandro lay back on his own towel, a lazy gaze on her, his head resting on one hand.

After a small hesitation she spread out her towel a good arm's length away and lay down on her stomach, her face hidden on folded arms. The sun played over her back, drying and warming her. At this time of day it wasn't too hot, although there was no wind.

Behind her closed lids she could still see an image of Zandro's magnificent body sprawled beside her, his eyes assessing her apparently casually but with a gleam of scarcely veiled male interest and appreciation. Nothing like the cruelly calculated offensiveness he'd subjected her to in the nursing home garden.

She shivered with a kind of pleasurable apprehension, and Zandro said, 'Are you cold?' Something trailed along her arm—the back of his fingers.

Involuntarily she raised her head, flinching from his touch. It was too tempting, too fraught with risk.

He was still watching her, had turned to rest an elbow on the sand. Withdrawing his hand, he cocked an eyebrow at her. 'I won't hurt you, Lia.'

The thought entered her mind with total clarity—*Yes you will, if I give you half a chance.* Especially if he ever found out about her duplicity. She had little doubt he'd be furious, and ruthless in his retribution. This gentler mood of his was surely an illusion—even a trap.

Shivering again, she twisted and sat up abruptly, ready to leave.

'You are cold,' he said.

'Yes.' Seizing the excuse, she made to get up.

'Don't run away.'

He moved, taking his own towel and draping it about her shoulders. It was slightly damp from his body, but the sun had heated the sand, and the rough fabric was warm.

Zandro smiled at her. 'Stay,' he said softly.

Conflicting emotions clashed inside her. Confusion, a sense of guilt at her own betrayal, her unwilling attraction to the enemy—and desire, brought to fever pitch by the faint smile lingering on his firm mouth, the glitter in his eyes that recognised her femininity, told her he liked looking at her. And that he too remembered the scorching kiss they'd shared.

'I don't frighten you, do I?' he said.

'No.' Untrue but she would never admit it. Not that she thought he would physically harm her, but she feared his sharp mind, his unbendable will, and she distrusted the sexual magnetism he unthinkingly—or perhaps intentionally—exerted. She forced scorn into her voice. 'Of course not.'

He smiled again, and she had the feeling he didn't believe her. 'You *have* changed,' he said meditatively. 'Sometimes you seem like a different person altogether from the Lia I knew before.'

The man was dangerously perceptive. Her heart thudding, she looked down at the sand, digging her toes into the warm grains. For her own good and for the success of her already hazardous plans she should keep away from him as much as possible. 'You never really knew me,' she said, an obstruction in her throat making her voice husky.

'Maybe not. I was more concerned with my brother, and later with Nicky.'

Lia had been way down his list of priorities. Lia had

been on her own with her bereavement, her pain. But…
'At least you looked after Nicky.'

'I tried to look after you too…for Rico's sake.'

She turned to see his face. 'Did you?' Hearing the faintly pleading note in her voice, she looked away again. 'Browbeating someone is not the right way to go about it.'

For a moment he said nothing. She shot another glance at him and found his brows pulled together. 'I'm sorry you saw it that way,' he said.

Her shoulder hunched in silent acknowledgement. Her toes curled and uncurled in the sand that now covered them. His new gentleness almost persuaded her that he really had been doing his best all those months ago—for both Nicky and Nicky's mother. Was it possible she could trust him?

But if she confessed, would he ever trust her?

She couldn't think with him so near. She stirred. 'I'm still cold.' She was, shivering inside. 'I'm going back to the house.'

She got to her feet, letting his towel drop from her shoulders, gathering up her own and winding it around her once more, ferociously tucking it in. And as Zandro got up, more slowly: 'You needn't come with me.'

He didn't answer, merely accompanying her as she climbed the short slope to the grass and hurried across it. This time she carefully checked for traffic on the road, and then had to wait for Zandro to open the gates.

'Was it your sister's death that made you decide to claim Nicky?' he asked as they went through.

Her gaze shot to his face, her eyes wide and apprehensive, and he went on, 'Because you have no other family left in the world?'

She swallowed a lump that had lodged in her throat.

'You think I'm that selfish? That I see him as some kind of live teddy bear, for my comfort?'

He frowned. 'Once I might have thought so. Now…I don't know. But it wouldn't be surprising if your judgment was influenced by grief.'

'This wasn't a sudden decision,' she said. 'I couldn't come before… My sister needed me.'

Once in the house she made towards her room, Zandro pacing beside her until she closed the door on him and leaned against it, feeling as if she'd just had some narrow escape. Not only from unwittingly giving herself away, but from something else—the emotional menace represented by Zandro Brunellesci. Especially when he was kind, when his eyes darkened with shocked sympathy and his voice gentled to a velvety, midnight note.

Zandro was the most unsettling man she'd ever met.

His compassion had seemed sincere, yet he immediately put his finger on any possible flaw in her intention to take Nicky away. Everything came back to that. The reason she was here was always uppermost in his thoughts—and in hers.

She crossed to her bathroom, dropped the damp, sandy towel into the laundry basket and as she straightened and glimpsed her reflection in a big mirror behind the door experienced a small involuntary thrill of pleasure, remembering how Zandro had studied and tacitly approved her body in the revealing swimsuit.

Quickly she turned away from the mirror and stripped off the clinging garment before stepping into the shower.

Deathly afraid of dropping her guard, she resolved to take the coward's way, retreat from a perilous, unwanted attraction, lock herself safely into her comfort zone and treat Zandro with an aloof courtesy akin to his father's manner to her.

She was chagrined when she put it into practice and he seemed to find it amusing, a faint smile lurking at the corners of his mouth while his gaze rested on her with a gleam of irritatingly tolerant perception. And something more. Something that made her heart beat faster, sent warm shivers chasing over her, in a kind of shamingly pleasurable agitation.

On Thursday when she entered the sitting room before dinner she learned guests were expected, and that Barbara wouldn't be joining them. Immediately she offered to eat her meal in the kitchen.

'No, no!' Mrs Brunellesci protested.

'Certainly not,' Zandro said, handing her a glass. 'You'll eat with us as usual.'

Even Domenico looked disapproving. 'We do not send our guests to eat in the kitchen.'

'But Barbara—'

'Her choice,' Zandro said.

Don't I get one? But before she could say anything the doorbell rang, and he excused himself and left the room. Minutes later he ushered in three people—two women and a man, all probably in their early thirties.

He introduced, 'Lia, who's staying with us for a while,' without any further information. The man was a wine merchant. One of the women, a magazine columnist, was his partner.

The other woman, a striking, dark-eyed brunette wearing a white sheath that showed off a stunning figure, was Rowena Hayes. The name and face were vaguely familiar, and when Zandro mentioned a TV programme the penny dropped. Rowena, a former model, was a 'personality' who appeared regularly in women's magazines also available on the other side of the Tasman Sea, and now hosted a popular local talk show.

At dinner Rowena was seated between Zandro and his father. Domenico unbent considerably in the face of her animated conversation accompanied by extravagant gestures and scintillating smiles. But she devoted most of her attention to his son. Her hair was loose and curling about her shoulders, and she had a habit of flipping it back with one hand, revealing a perfect profile as she turned to speak with Zandro.

Most men would have been dazzled. Zandro retained his usual self-possession but there was warmth in his eyes when he looked at her. During the dessert course she fixed her sparkling gaze on him yet again and murmured something too low for the others to hear. He inclined his head closer to catch the words, then gave her a slow smile and returned an equally low-voiced reply that she received with a laugh, touching his hand where it lay on the table, and casting him a provocative glance from under fabulous lashes.

They were flirting. There was no reason to be irritated by that. Maybe they even had a relationship. Zandro might not have committed himself to marriage, but a man with so much going for him was unlikely to have abstained from female company. On Monday night he'd been out for dinner, and still hadn't come in when the rest of the household had retired to bed.

'What do you do, Lia?'

Her mind still occupied with speculation about Zandro and Rowena, it was a moment before she turned to the male half of the couple, seated at her side. 'Sorry?'

'I was asking what you do for a living.'

'I'm a librarian,' she said automatically.

Zandro gave her a sharp look across the table. 'I thought you were in the travel industry.'

A stupid slip to make. She picked up a piece of meat with her fork. 'For a while.' Turning to her neighbour again, she began to question him about the Australian wine trade and almost managed to forget the couple at the other side of the table, except when she heard Zandro's quiet laughter, Rowena's intimate tone. An inexplicable urge to slap them both made her tighten her hold on her knife.

She was relieved when dinner was over and they moved to the other room for coffee. Zandro ensconced Rowena on a sofa and went to help his mother who was pouring. He handed a cup to Rowena, then said, 'Lia? A liqueur…or just coffee?'

She shook her head, coming to a decision. 'Thanks, but I don't think so. I'll leave you with your guests.'

She said goodnight to the others and left the room, aware that for some reason Zandro was annoyed with her. He should, she thought, have been glad to get rid of the spare wheel of an extra woman so he could concentrate on entertaining his celebrity girlfriend.

The memory of that kiss in the nursing home gardens resurfaced. If he was involved with Rowena, she told herself angrily, he had no right to be kissing other women.

Zandro Brunellesci was an enigma. In the business world he was known for astuteness and toughness. At home he showed a different personality, respectful of his father though not afraid to stand up to him when they disagreed, a loving son to his mother, gentle with Nicky, always courteous to the household employees, even deferring to Barbara's experienced judgment in matters of child care.

Yet she had stark knowledge of his ruthless streak, his lack of understanding of his own brother or compassion for the bereaved mother of Rico's child.

She went to the darkened nursery first. Nicky slept with one arm about a toy rabbit, the other dimpled hand resting on the sheet. He looked angelic, as she supposed all sleeping babies did, and her heart swelled with love for him.

This defenceless little person was her responsibility, a sacred trust she couldn't evade or shuck off. Whatever the rights and wrongs of the situation, however frightening the web of lies and half-truths and muddled good intentions winding tighter and tighter about her, she must hold on to the one thing that mattered.

Silently she lowered the side of the cot until she could bend down and kiss a warm, soft cheek. Nicky didn't even stir, and after a moment she replaced the safety barrier and crept from the room.

She lay sleepless in her bed. The guests left late, car doors slamming, voices carrying upward through the open window—Zandro's unmistakable deep tones, a light laugh from Rowena.

Were they close? Did Zandro think of marrying her? He might consider marriage, if only to strengthen his claim to Nicky. A married couple could have a better chance of being given custody by a court than a single woman, if it ever came to that.

Would a TV star accustomed to a public life make a good mother?

Unfair, she told herself, to judge the woman by one

evening in her company. Fame didn't preclude normal maternal instinct.

The cars outside purred away through the gate and the front door closed, then there was silence.

Tug-of-love children always aroused sympathy. They tore at one's heart, those poor little pawns in the miserable games of the grown-ups.

How had she involved herself in this no-win situation? Why?

She'd been persuaded by a desperate dying request.

But it was more than that. *You were consumed with guilt,* an inner voice whispered. *You wanted to make up for what you'd not done. Atonement.*

Thinking of the oblivious little boy asleep along the passageway, she tried to put aside her own emotions and look dispassionately at the apparently insoluble problem. How could she leave him to the Brunellescis, whom their own son and brother had repudiated, let them warp his life and turn him into an unhappy, resentful adult?

Yet how could she take him away to a different country, from the only home and family he knew, wrench him from the comfort and security he was already accustomed to? Zandro wasn't likely to let her get away with it easily; he'd try to find them. And a life on the run with a mother looking over her shoulder all the time couldn't be good for a child.

Footfalls sounded outside her door, then another noise brought her to full alertness. Surely that was Nicky? A high, muffled cry, followed by another, sharper and louder.

Out of bed in a flash, she left her room and hurried down the dimly lit passageway.

The door to Nicky's room was open. A large dark

figure bent over his cot. She heard the murmur of Zandro's voice mixed with the baby's continuing wail.

Barbara appeared at his side, fastening a robe. 'Shall I—'

Zandro bent and picked up the baby, holding it close against his shoulder. 'It's okay, Barbara,' he said quietly without turning. 'I'll call if he needs you.'

The nanny hesitated, then went back to her bedroom. Zandro hadn't noticed that she wasn't the only woman who'd responded to Nicky's distress. He was rubbing Nicky's back, and at last turned towards the door. 'Lia?'

She moved into the room. 'I heard him crying.'

The sobs were already abating. Nicky's hand clutched at Zandro's shirt, his face resting on the man's shoulder. 'Dee,' he murmured sleepily. A small hand touched Zandro's chin.

Zandro's teeth showed briefly in a smile. His palm tenderly cradled the baby's head, and he kissed the dark curls, then laid the back of his fingers against a rounded cheek. 'He isn't hot. Maybe it was a dream.'

'The visitors may have woken him when they left.' She watched Nicky's body slump against the white linen of Zandro's shirt, saw a slight flutter of the amazingly long, dark lashes on one eyelid, then it stilled. 'I think he's asleep again,' she whispered.

Zandro didn't relinquish his tiny burden immediately. 'Did they wake you?' he asked very quietly, his breath stirring Nicky's curls.

'No, I wasn't sleeping.'

His head rose a little but the light wasn't strong enough to pick up his expression. 'You left us very early.'

He sounded disapproving. She didn't answer, merely lifting a shoulder.

Zandro looked down at Nicky again and shifted his grip, before very carefully placing the little boy back into his cot, pulling the covers over him and tucking them in. He didn't need to lower the side to stoop and touch his lips to the child's forehead, then he stayed for several seconds just watching his nephew sleep. 'He's very like his father,' he commented quietly, and she heard a new, grating note in his voice.

'Your mother said so,' she recalled. 'She told me Rico was a happy little boy. But you…you said he was spoiled.'

'That didn't stop me loving him.' He turned to her then. 'Everyone loved Rico.'

Some note in his voice of bitterness emboldened her to say, 'Did you think they couldn't love you as much?'

In the darkness she was unable to read his face, but a slight movement of his body betrayed some restless emotion. 'Could you?' he asked strangely, and then without apparently expecting an answer, he laughed quietly, and said, 'We both know how Rico was. How could you help but fall in love with him?'

An unanswerable question, and fortunately a rhetorical one. After a moment of silence, Zandro moved away from the cot, took her arm and led her from the room, pulling the door almost to behind them.

He dropped his hand, and his gaze took in the short, thin cotton nightshirt, lingering on the point where her thighs emerged from the hem. Then he raised his eyes and lifted a hand to cup her chin. 'Goodnight, Lia,' he said, and quickly bent his head, his lips capturing hers in a warm, firm kiss before he drew away.

He laid a finger over her lips, which were parted in

surprise, then he stepped back and turned, rapidly making for his own room. He had closed the door without looking back before she could force herself to move and return to her bed.

Zandro might have envied his brother's sunnier nature, his easy road through childhood, his capacity for inviting affection, but like his parents Zandro had also known grief when Rico was snatched from them.

They must have found some comfort in caring for Rico's son. Mrs Brunellesci's love for Nicky was obvious, and surely there could no longer be any doubt about Zandro's. A love that was trustingly, innocently returned.

She'd seen the baby fearlessly approach Domenico, who would absentmindedly take the little boy on his knee, patiently letting Nicky pat his face and inquisitively inspect his clothing or the rings he wore on two of his fingers, and sometimes snuggle down sleepily against his grandfather's chest.

She tossed restlessly until dawn, and then got up and with tears running unheeded down her cheeks, when the sun gilded the water and split apart the grey cloud on the horizon, came to a decision.

Next evening Zandro didn't appear at dinner, and Mrs Brunellesci said he'd been detained at the office. After a blustery day with intermittent showers, Nicky had been unusually fractious before Barbara put him to bed a little early and came down for the meal.

The nanny had drunk her coffee and gone upstairs before Zandro appeared, wearing his business suit and looking particularly austere, more like his father than ever as he stopped in the doorway of the sitting room.

His mother greeted him, offering coffee, but he

shook his head. 'No, thank you, Mamma.' Shifting his gaze, he said with a kind of distant chill, 'I want to speak with you…Lia.' And to his parents, 'You'll excuse us, please.'

Mrs Brunellesci showed surprise at his curtness, and his father gave him a keenly curious perusal, but Zandro wasn't looking at them. 'Lia?' His tone was peremptory. 'We'll talk in my study.'

She had been relieved that he wasn't home, and now was tempted to refuse the headmasterly order, noting with trepidation the harsh line of his lips, the angle of his strong jaw. But she had to talk to him sometime, and putting it off wouldn't remove the leaden lump that seemed to have taken the place of her heart.

'What about?' she asked, carefully placing her empty cup on a side table. Her heart was thumping unnaturally and when she finally stood up her knees felt weak.

'I don't think you'll want to discuss it here,' he said forbiddingly.

His father frowned but said nothing. Mrs Brunellesci apparently decided to follow his example.

Zandro stood back with a slight bow and a wave of his hand, indicating that his victim should precede him, the gesture so subtly exaggerated that she couldn't accuse him of deliberate satire though she was sure it was a mockery of genuine courtesy. Walking along the passageway to a room she'd never been in before, she felt as if she were being followed by a jailer.

He switched on the light when they entered, and closed the door behind them. The room contained a large desk with a laptop computer and printer on it, an office chair behind it, and two comfortable armchairs. Books and papers were neatly arrayed on floor-to-ceiling shelves. Obviously some serious work took place here.

'Sit down,' Zandro said, remaining in front of the door as if barring any attempt at escape.

'No.' She turned to face him, not wanting to sit if he planned to remain standing. 'What's this all about?'

'I might well ask you that question.' His face seemed a little paler than usual, and she sensed he was holding himself tightly in check, his whole stance indicating strain. She didn't need to be a genius to deduce that underneath the calm exterior he was seething, ominously furious.

Her heart plunged with dread, but she told herself not to jump to conclusions. Better let him get whatever it was out of the way—and put off the evil moment when she said what she had to say. 'I don't know what you're talking about.'

The rigid mask slipped and a flare of temper lit his eyes. He took a step towards her and she had to clench her fists and stiffen her back to stop herself retreating, cowering in a corner. 'Don't stuff about with me,' he said. 'The game's up. I don't know how you ever thought you'd get away with it.'

'With…what?' Of course she knew, but stupidly she clung to a ridiculous hope that she'd have a chance to explain, give her side of the story and make him understand before he condemned her for what she was— a liar and a cheat.

Zandro came closer, his eyes lancing into hers, accusing and condemning. 'This farcical charade of yours,' he said, his voice harsh and unforgiving.

Her head was going to explode, she thought dazedly, either before or after she threw up on the expensively carpeted floor. Somehow she swallowed down the nausea, her eyes fixed on the dark, accusing ones that held her silent and heart-plungingly fearful.

'Lia Cameron died two months ago,' Zandro said grittily, his gaze holding no trace of pity or understanding, 'leaving only one surviving member of her family—her twin sister, Cara.'

CHAPTER SEVEN

'You,' Zandro ground out. 'You're Cara, aren't you?' Without waiting for an answer he seized her face in one large hand, his fingers hard, and inspected her with merciless eyes. 'If I'd known Lia and her sister were twins I might have suspected—you seemed so different—but Rico never mentioned that interesting fact. And neither did she.'

'How—how did you find out?' she managed to say.

He dropped his hand. 'I've had a private detective investigating you—or rather, Lia—ever since you turned up here.'

Hoping, she supposed, to strengthen his case for continuing guardianship. Why hadn't she thought of that? 'I...I was going to tell you,' she said, but even in her own ears it sounded feeble, unconvincing. She would never persuade him now that last night she'd finally accepted there was no way she could justify removing Nicky from this family.

He belonged with his grandparents—the only ones he had—with his cousins who adored him, and his uncle who loved him and had looked after him as best he knew how. She could only hope to have a small influence on his upbringing, and be there for him whenever he felt the need of someone connected with his mother. A hope that Zandro was now going to be less than ever inclined to fulfil.

Something other than cold rage entered his expression. Contempt—disbelief. 'When?' he shot at her.

'T-tonight, probably.' Cara swallowed. 'You see, Lia—' She stopped, trying to keep tears at bay.

He saw them. 'I'm sorry you lost your sister,' he told her, a bare hint of compassion tempering his angry gaze, the harshness in his voice. 'If you'd *come* to us,' he said with controlled ferocity, 'we'd have made some arrangement for you to have contact—but this deception…*why?*'

'Because Lia wanted me to have Nicky! And Rico never wanted his son to be treated the way *he* was.'

Zandro's composure cracked, dark eyes blazing so that she took a step back. 'Rico was treated like a bloody prince! I told you, my mother adored him, even my father let him get away with murder when he was a kid. They did *everything* for him.'

His vehemence sparked her previous suspicion into certainty. 'You *were* jealous of him!' she said.

'As a child? No.' He repudiated the idea impatiently. 'The other way 'round, perhaps.' His expression turned bleak.

'The *other* way?' she echoed.

A shoulder lifted. 'One of the things he flung at us before he left home in a temper was that my father needn't bother any more to hide his preference for his favourite son—me. The one who was happy to follow in our father's footsteps. Or be his footstool.'

She could almost laugh at that—Zandro was nobody's footstool and never would be. Strangely, this new light on their family relationships accorded with her own recent reflections on the difference between Rico and his brother.

'Apparently,' Zandro went on, 'he felt my father's willingness to let my mother give into him was rooted in indifference rather than love. And when he—my father—tried to remedy his negligence, and enlisted my help, it was too late.'

According to her sister, they'd been determined to force Rico into a mould he wasn't fitted for.

'No one meant to make him unhappy,' Zandro said. 'I've tried to make it up to him through his son. But I don't suppose I can make you understand.'

She understood perfectly. Too much so for her peace of mind. His dilemma woke uncomfortable echoes in her own psyche.

But... 'That wasn't how Lia saw it. She came home sick and bereaved and heartbroken. And saying it was all your fault.'

'You believe that?' Zandro seemed to grow even taller, his eyes laserlike, scorching.

Cara hesitated. 'I don't know,' she admitted, her voice low, feeling she was betraying her sister. 'You took her baby—'

'You know why!'

'I didn't, then. She told me she was given painkillers and sleeping pills in hospital while she was recovering, and that they helped to blot out her grief at Rico's death. Afterwards she couldn't do without them. But she was determined to shake off her need for them and get her baby back...'

'Did she tell you,' Zandro demanded, 'that Rico had a cocktail of illegal drugs in his system when he crashed their car?'

Numbly Cara shook her head. 'The accident was a blank in her memory.' Lia had suffered concussion as well as other injuries. 'She was only thankful that Dominic—Nicky—was safe in his car seat and not hurt.' With anguish, she added, 'If only she'd contacted me then!' Losing Rico in so similar a manner to her parents' deaths must have been more than traumatic. 'I knew nothing until she came home.'

'Nothing? She didn't keep in touch?' His tone was doubting.

'Sometimes.' Remembered hurt made her voice husky. 'But after she met Rico…'

Cara had told herself she was glad her sister had found the man she'd rhapsodised was her soul mate. And tried not to feel abandoned when the infrequent postcards and phone calls dwindled still further. Or when Cara phoned and after an effusive greeting Lia began to sound distracted and vague, as though the conversation bored her and she was thinking of something else. Sometimes Rico's voice was audible in the background, the words indistinguishable but the tone coaxing or laughing. Lia had always been the one to terminate the call.

'You didn't have an inkling anything was wrong?'

Something stuck in her throat, and she cleared it. 'I wanted to come over,' she said, 'when Lia got pregnant, but she said to wait until the baby was born.' She paused to steady her voice. 'I didn't like to intrude.' She blanked out the reason why she'd felt unable to do so, continuing, 'It was natural for her to look to the father of her baby for support.'

'You were better informed than we were,' Zandro rasped. 'We knew nothing about any baby until the hospital called to tell us Rico had died. My parents were listed as his next of kin on a card they found. My mother took the call.'

Poor Mrs Brunellesci.

'Lia was in and out of consciousness,' Zandro said, 'but she wouldn't let us bring the baby home, and later she discharged herself and walked out with him. When

I found her again she was in a squalid little flat with a couple of other…people. The place was filthy, over-crowded and barely furnished, and the neighbours banged on the walls when Nicky cried—which seemed to be pretty constantly.'

Cara swallowed again, painfully. 'Aren't you exag-gerating?' she accused without conviction.

'No. I had to threaten to report the situation to the authorities to persuade her to come here with Nicky.'

Wouldn't Lia have contacted her if things had been that bad? Given some hint that she was in dire trouble? But then, Cara hadn't even known about the accident or Rico's death until her sister was back home.

Something seemed to have hollowed out her insides. 'I got no reply when I phoned, and later the phone was cut off. I was worried, but when she finally called she said she'd moved and was busy with the baby, and that when everything was settled I must come over.' A clear hint that a premature visit would be unwelcome. '*Why* didn't she say something? She knew I'd help her!'

'She didn't want help. I tried, God knows.'

'But *I* wouldn't have taken her baby from her! I'm her sister!'

'Maybe she didn't want you to know what a mess she'd made of her life over here.'

Cara closed her eyes, then forced them open again. 'She wanted to be independent after our parents died.' Her voice was close to a whisper. 'That's why she came to Australia. Alone.'

In a different environment, away from reminders of loss and grief, she'd start anew, Lia had said. Unlike Cara, who had found some comfort in living in the family home surrounded by mementoes of their parents, Lia had needed to distance herself from the reminders.

Cara had immediately said she'd come, too, afraid of letting her sister take such a step on her own, still grieving as she was for their parents. 'At least wait a while,' she'd urged. But Lia was adamant.

They'd had one of their rare quarrels. The worst ever. Cara's mind skittered away from the unbearable memory.

'She did come to you in the end,' Zandro said.

'After she'd overdosed on sleeping pills.' Or had it been something stronger? Cara felt disloyal even as the pernicious thought entered her mind.

'You must have wondered why she didn't bring Nicky with her?' A deep frown furrowed the skin between his brows.

Did he doubt her word? If so it wasn't surprising—she had after all been deceiving him and his family ever since their first meeting. 'I assumed she was bringing him until I met her at the airport. When I saw her…' Everything else had vanished from her mind.

The woman she'd met at the airport had been barely recognisable, thin and pale and with her hair cut shockingly short, a style that only emphasised ghastly hollowed cheeks and the blue-tinged skin under lifeless eyes. 'She didn't tell me what had happened to Rico and Nicky until I got her home.' Cara hadn't dared ask questions before that.

Then Lia poured it all out, amid tears and racking sobs that had gone on for hours, until exhaustion claimed her and Cara half carried her to bed.

Then she'd made herself coffee and sat down to absorb all that her sister had told her—including that

Zandro Brunellesci had virtually forced Lia to give up her baby.

'It wasn't easy for her, stopping the pills. And…the overdose had damaged her liver. There was nothing the doctors could do. At the end she had to have something for the pain, though she held out against it as long as she could.'

Cara shivered, wound her arms about herself and turned away, dashing the back of her hand across her eyes.

He laid a hand on her shoulder and she tried to shrug it off, but Zandro grasped the other shoulder and brought her around to face him.

She had to look up into his eyes, dark and fathomless and unreadable. 'Did you really try to help her?' she entreated.

'Every way I could.' The words held conviction that she couldn't discount. 'I set up counselling sessions for her but she stopped attending. It turned out she'd found a supplier here and had been visiting him instead.'

'A…supplier?'

His voice roughened. 'She couldn't get all those pills legally, Cara. Even if harder drugs weren't involved.'

Closing her eyes, Cara tried to absorb that. Her legs felt weak and, as if he knew, Zandro drew her into his arms, held her.

Suddenly tired, she rested her head on his shoulder, her hands against his chest. It felt comforting, secure. Strange, because he despised her again now, condemned her duplicity.

Lia had lied to her…at least by omission. 'I can't believe it,' she muttered into Zandro's shirt, even as the dread certainty grew into a black weight taking up residence in her stomach. She had tried so hard not to believe those dreadful things of her sister. Then, horrified, she lifted her head. 'If she was on drugs while she was pregnant with Nicky...'

His gaze was steady, reassuring but cool. 'I had a doctor check him over and there seemed to be no lasting ill effects. With my mother and a part-time nurse to make sure he was properly fed and looked after, he thrived.'

'Lia wouldn't have endangered her baby,' Cara argued. 'She was *shattered* that he'd been taken from her. Suicidal.'

At the angry lift of her chin, the fire in her eyes, he said swiftly, 'Addicts have a skewed view of the world. Nothing is as important as their next dose of whatever poison has taken them over. Very possibly the baby didn't even seem real to her until he was actually born.'

That hit home; Cara recalled her sister saying almost the same words.

'Before or after,' Zandro went on, 'she wasn't capable of putting his needs first.'

'She did, when you convinced her he'd be better off without her!'

Cara stirred in his arms but he didn't loosen his hold. 'Not until I offered her money.'

'No!' It was a protest rather than a denial, her head tilted until she could see his face. 'You're saying she sold her child!'

He looked pensive, considering, his eyes not wavering from hers. 'I suppose she loved him in her way, but Lia couldn't be trusted, Cara. She'd put him on the changing table, turn away to find talcum or a nappy, and just wander off. Then she tried to take the baby and run away. I wasn't going to let her ruin his life as well as hers. I couldn't *make* her stick to a treatment programme, but I could save Nicky. And I was prepared to use any means in my power to do that.'

Cara shivered. He had gone about it quite ruthlessly, she was sure. That much Lia hadn't been lying about. 'You threatened her...'

'With exposing her habit and her inadequacy as a mother to the authorities, yes. Gave her a choice between them or signing over Nicky's guardianship to me. But what finally swayed her was the offer of hard cash to go away and not have any contact with Nicky...' A tinge of regret softened his features. 'Although I knew I was throwing her back into that half-life she'd led with Rico.'

'But without him! How could you—'

'I had to think of Nicky!' His eyes briefly flared. 'The last straw was when she screamed at the nurse we'd hired, snatched Nicky and locked herself in her room with him. He was terrified, and we had no idea what she might do. When we finally got to them she attacked my mother—hit her. My father wanted to throw her out of the house there and then. I couldn't allow that sort of thing to continue. It was bad for the baby, and unsafe.'

He couldn't be making all this up.

Cara had arrived in Australia believing Zandro was a cold-hearted monster, but living with him for even a short time had shown her he was human after all. And he had a code of integrity that she was deep-down certain wouldn't allow him to stoop to lying, slandering a dead woman who could no longer defend herself. She swallowed a lump rising in her throat. Her chest hurt, and something thudded at her temples. She closed her eyes again.

'You'd better sit down,' Zandro said abruptly. 'You're pale.'

She let him lead her to a chair, and he stood before her, frowning, his hands in his pockets.

'Whose crazy idea was this imposture of yours?' His anger had abated for a while but now it flared again in his eyes.

'Lia's.' Cara had immediately vetoed it, but Lia had been frantic, hysterical. And dying. 'I told her I'd apply for custody, but she said a single woman against your family and the lawyers you could afford wouldn't have a prayer. I knew she was right.'

'What were you going to do, supposing it had worked? Pretend to be your sister for the rest of your life?' he said dismissively. 'You were bound to get found out eventually.'

'I intended to disappear with Nicky,' she confessed, not surprised at the tightening of his mouth, the renewed flash of anger in his eyes. 'Go someplace where we weren't known. Maybe change my name.'

'I'd have found you.' He looked implacable, dangerous. 'Found Nicky. Make no mistake about that.'

She didn't. He'd have moved heaven and earth, used all his considerable power to come after her. She'd been mad to ever imagine she could escape him.

He swung away from her, thrusting a hand over his hair, then when he reached the desk turned to face her again. 'You're not even his real mother!' Accusing.

'I know.' All the guilt she'd been fighting last night threatened to crush her. 'Lia…and Rico—'

'Rico would not have wanted his son brought up by a stranger.'

'He wouldn't—didn't—want him brought up by his family. He hadn't even told you about Nicky!'

Zandro's lips pressed together again, containing the temper he was determinedly holding by a thin leash. 'And that hurt my mother very much. Her first grandson…'

'Lia said—'

He made a cutting gesture with his hand. 'Lia was hardly a reliable witness. My father may have been harsh at times, shown his disappointment by losing his temper. He's Italian and not given to hiding his feelings. But this crazy scheme… What the hell were you thinking?'

'I was thinking of Nicky,' she said, suddenly immeasurably weary. Relieved that the strain of pretence was over, depressed at what she couldn't help feeling was a failure of her mission.

Rico had exaggerated to Lia the family preoccupation with money at the expense of relationships, and Lia had believed him, passed on that belief to Cara. And lied about her own culpability. 'I suppose you'll throw me out now.' She was here under false pretences, after all. 'But I'm not about to give up all contact with Nicky.' Rallying herself, she tried to sound assertive. 'I *am* his aunt.'

'Throw you out?' Apparently the thought hadn't occurred to him. 'That wouldn't solve anything.' He paused. 'And if you still have any ideas about kidnapping him, put them right out of your mind. I'd hunt you down and make sure you regretted it for the rest of your life.'

He was starkly, unmistakably threatening her. It threw her right back to her first misgivings about him. 'This is what Lia warned me about,' she said, her eyes lifting accusingly despite an inward tremor. 'You've no need to bully me. You've won. Isn't that enough?'

'I'll protect my family with any means at my disposal,' he said. 'And Nicky is family. If that makes me a bully, so is every man who keeps the people he loves from harm.'

'I wouldn't harm Nicky! And I won't try to take him away. Even though—' her voice shook '—it means breaking my promise to my sister.'

'Deathbed promises are emotional blackmail,' Zandro observed bitingly. 'They should never be regarded as binding on anyone.'

'I had to do it. Lia was desperate. But…it was wrong. I told you, I'd realised that before you found out…' It didn't seem to matter now whether he believed her or not. She closed her eyes, shutting out his condemning gaze, then forced them open again.

'You're exhausted,' he said, his tones clipped as though sympathy was against his better judgment. 'Why don't you go to bed, and I'll explain to my parents.'

She stood up. '*I* should do that.' She ought to ask their forgiveness.

His eyes searched her face. 'Do you really want to?' He was quite close, not moving away.

'No, but—'

'I won't paint you as the wicked impostor.' He gave her a curious, smouldering look. 'Were you really prepared to perjure yourself?'

'I hoped I wouldn't have to go that far.'

He didn't reply, going to the door and opening it to signal the interview was over. When she reached him he took her shoulders again and kissed her mouth—a strange, hard kiss. Brief and electrifying.

A wave of heat, unmistakable sexual hunger travelled all the way to her toes. But when she stared up at him as he released her, his eyes still held a banked glow of anger mingled with naked, primitive desire. 'I don't appreciate being made a fool of,' he said, his voice gravelly. As if the kiss had been some kind of retribution.

She understood. Somehow his rage was mixed with passion, both emotions heightened by the fraught circumstances—and he didn't like it or understand it any more than she did.

Then he was giving her a small push towards the stairs. 'Go on,' he said. 'I'll handle this.'

He could handle anything. She went up the stairs and into Nicky's room, staying there for a long time—watching him sleep, listening to his breathing. He was all she had left of her beloved sister.

'She loved you,' Cara whispered, fingering one stray curl from the smooth baby forehead. 'Your mummy loved you very much.'

Yet she'd left him with the Brunellescis. Lia wouldn't have done that unless deep down she'd known that Nicky was safe with them. Perhaps safer than with his own mother, even if she hadn't wanted to admit it.

Breakfast was awkward. When Cara entered the room Domenico turned to her with haughty censure in his face, and Mrs Brunellesci looked confused and embarrassed. Zandro got up to pull out a chair, but before she sat down Cara said, 'I'm sorry I lied to you all, but for my sister's sake I felt I had no choice.'

Domenico merely gave a stiff nod, then said, 'We regret your sister's death.'

His wife looked up at Zandro before sending Cara a small, anxious smile. 'A very sad loss.' Then she glanced at her son, who had settled himself back into his own chair after seating Cara. 'Zandro says you can't take him away from us.'

Before Cara could reply, Zandro said, 'You have no need to worry, Mamma. Nicky is ours.'

'He's my sister's son,' Cara said.

'And my brother's,' Zandro reminded her.

Mrs Brunellesci said, 'He is Cara's *nipote,* Zandro. And yours.'

'We will discuss this later,' Zandro decreed. 'And come to some arrangement.'

She ought, Cara supposed, to be thankful. Zandro might have won but he was prepared to be magnanimous.

In the evening when Zandro returned from the office she asked to speak to him in his study.

'I could move to Australia,' she said, 'live nearby. I hope you won't oppose that.' She tried to keep the pleading note from her voice, though she was aware she was at a disadvantage. But for Nicky she would go on her knees and beg if necessary.

Zandro was removing his jacket, taking off his tie. 'You said once that visiting rights weren't enough.'

'I suppose it's all I can expect now. But—' her chin lifted '—if I think Nicky is being in any way abused, physically or emotionally, I warn you I'll take it to court and fight you for custody.'

'You'd lose.' His voice was cutting. 'Nicky will never be abused in this house.'

She saw the slight flutter of the material of his shirt as he breathed in, then out again. His gaze became almost meditative, fixed on her. Something in it changed, taking on a disturbing intensity, and the air seemed to close in, making Cara's skin feel hot and oversensitive as if a warm wind were passing over her. His throat moved, and his mouth softened infinitesimally from its habitual firm lines. His beautiful male lips parted very slightly, the tip of his tongue briefly touching them.

Her heartbeat accelerated. The warmth on her skin spread inside her, coursing through her body. 'What?' she said, trying to mentally break away from him. But she didn't move, mesmerised by the light burning in his eyes, the sheer male force of him. The man was a walking aphrodisiac—unsafe at any distance.

'I have an idea,' he said abruptly. 'A solution.'

Cara stiffened. It entered her mind that he was quite deliberately using his considerable sexual magnetism to persuade her into something she might regret. With an effort she took a step away, an attempt to escape that seductive aura.

He reached for her, his hands closing about her upper arms. 'Listen.' He paused, and for a moment she thought doubt, uncertainty, entered his eyes. Then he said, 'There's one way out of this dilemma, if you agree.'

Warily she stared at him. She mustn't be influenced by the effect he had on her, the physical responses that clamoured to be set free from the stern restraint she kept on them. 'Agree to what?'

He was looking at her as though willing her to something, his gaze hypnotic. His jaw jutted, and she saw the muscles of his throat move as he swallowed. He said, 'To marry me.'

CHAPTER EIGHT

CARA'S mouth fell open in shock. She closed it again, her mind reeling. Had she heard that right? Finally she managed to make her voice work, although it sounded weak and hoarse. 'M-*marry* you?'

'It will resolve the problem,' he said. 'We adopt Nicky as a couple. Equal rights, equal responsibility. You get to bring him up as you promised, and he remains a part of my family, living in the family home. That way he has the best of all worlds.'

'But…we don't even know each other. Until yesterday you thought I was someone else!'

'I knew you weren't the same woman I'd known before.'

'You guessed?'

'No, I believed that the woman who turned up here was Lia. I thought maybe she'd kicked her habit and rediscovered her real self—responsible, considerate…loving. When I discovered the truth everything fell into place.'

And he'd realised then that Cara had no more right to Nicky than he did.

Mustering some will, she pushed out of his hold and put more distance between them. 'Marriage?' She shook her head, then had to raise a hand to brush a wayward strand of hair from her eyes. Surely it was a crazy idea. 'A convenient arrangement for Nicky's sake? What would you get out of it?'

He seemed to consider his answer, and when he

spoke his voice was even and quite dispassionate. His eyelids lowered, hiding what was behind them. 'I always intended to marry one day,' he said. 'Didn't you?'

'You want to marry a stranger?'

His head tilted to one side. 'I know quite a lot about you, Cara.'

Something chilled her spine. 'Your detective? He won't have found anything I'm ashamed of.'

'No,' Zandro said, 'he didn't. You were a good student—better than your sister. You studied humanities at university. She dabbled in art and left before getting a degree, went into advertising, did a bit of modelling, then worked in the travel business. You did a postgraduate diploma in librarianship and worked in a public library until you resigned to care for Lia.' He paused. 'You had a boyfriend who seems to have faded from the picture after Lia came home.'

'I was too tired and stressed to be with him much, certainly not to be good company.' Remembered hurt made her blink, stemming incipient tears. 'I don't blame him for getting sick of it.'

'If he wasn't man enough to stand by you when you were going through a difficult experience, he was no loss.'

A brutal assessment, although probably true. At the time she'd felt guilty for having neglected their relationship, and for a while she'd missed him dreadfully. Loyal, sympathetic female friends helped fill the gap, but it would have been nice sometimes to have a broad male shoulder to lean on while she wept at the imminent loss of her beloved sister. A shoulder like Zandro's, that he'd offered her last night despite his simmering fury. 'Lia was more important,' she said.

'That's something else I know about you,' he said. 'You're prepared to sacrifice alot, fight any threat, for those you love—you're intensely protective.'

She shrugged, uncomfortable at the personal analysis.

'You love the sea, you like your coffee with a smidgen of sugar, you have a nice singing voice—' At her start of surprise, he said, 'I've heard you singing to Nicky.'

She hadn't known he was around at those times. 'And,' he went on, 'you get on well with people. Barbara's quite a fan, and my family were surprised. You're good with children—Nicky's cousins took to you, though you didn't fuss over them. You have long showers…' He laughed at her widened eyes. 'Your bathroom is next to mine. And you come out smelling of violets and apples.' In his eyes a wicked spark appeared, and his voice had lowered to a seductive note, his gaze slipping over her, veiled by his thick black lashes.

'Soap and shampoo,' she said faintly, certain that he was picturing her in the shower. Her body was suddenly hot, trembly. 'All that doesn't amount to knowing a person.'

'It helps. I know your opinion on most current issues, and your concern for children's rights and animal welfare.'

They'd discussed all of them, after the TV news in the evening, or over dinner. Even at the breakfast table. She supposed she knew quite a lot about his opinions and habits too, had been surprised that he shared some of her views, her tastes.

'You're a compassionate person,' he said. 'You nursed your sister devotedly through her terminal illness, and you even feel for perfect strangers, people you see mentioned in the newspapers, or on the TV. I've seen it in your face.'

'You've been studying me,' she said uneasily. Scouting the enemy, surely, not with the idea of taking her as his wife. 'But this…' She shook her head.

'It's a sensible solution. Everybody wins. But let's be clear on one thing. I don't envisage a cold-blooded arrangement. Convenient, maybe, but there are enough sparks between us to make it—' he paused '—exhilarating.'

She'd have been a fool to think he was proposing a sexless relationship. A man who carried as much masculine appeal as he did would hardly settle for celibacy. Unless… 'Don't you have a girlfriend?' she asked. Not that she was seriously considering this outrageous scheme. The question had slipped out.

He looked at her thoughtfully. 'Not right now.'

Had he just ditched Rowena? Or had they only been on the brink of a relationship when they'd flirted over the dinner table? She was trying to frame a question when he said, 'And I won't have any after I'm married. I consider marriage a sacred and binding contract, *forsaking all others*. There'll be no other woman in my life.' His eyes darkened and met hers in unmistakable warning. 'And I expect no other man in yours. You won't make a fool of me again.'

'I haven't said I'll marry you!'

'You don't need to make up your mind tonight. Think about it. And while you're doing so—' he strolled closer to her '—think about this.'

He enfolded her in his arms, and when she went rigid and tense, he said softly, 'Relax, Cara. There's nothing to fear.'

'I'm not—'

The words were cut off as he bent his head and kissed her—expertly, a fact she registered and tried to resent, but his mouth was working such magic that within seconds she couldn't think at all, simply lost in the sensations he aroused, the scent of him, the feel of his body close to hers, his arms holding her firmly but with care.

The kiss lasted a long time, and he ran a hand almost experimentally over her before it settled on her breast—*inspecting the goods,* she thought in a desperate moment of clear-headed cynicism. He kissed her more deeply, with open, demanding passion, and then he closed his teeth gently on her lower lip before drawing back to study her flushed face.

There was colour in his cheeks too, intensifying the glitter in his eyes.

He still held her, and she tried to gather herself, fighting a longing to throw her arms about his neck and caution to the winds. Her lips felt full and moist, and she trembled as he slid his hand from her breast and linked both his hands behind her, smiling at her in a way that reminded her of some feral animal with its prey in sight.

He said, 'I wanted to do that the first time I saw you, when I yanked you out of the car and you looked at me as if I were Mephistopheles himself.'

She blinked. 'You *what?*' Her hands, laid against his chest to push him away, stilled in surprise.

'I couldn't understand it.' His grin was crooked, a line appearing between his brows. 'I'd never had the slightest desire to kiss Lia before. It's a wonder I didn't twig sooner that you weren't her.'

'We look exactly alike.'

'The differences are subtle but real—in expression, gesture…certainly in character.'

'You didn't know her—not the real Lia.'

'Perhaps not. But I know she was fortunate in having a sister like you. As I'll be fortunate if you agree to be my wife…and Nicky's mother.'

Was this supposed to persuade her into going along with his bizarre plan? 'You're not in love with me!' She did push against him then, and he reluctantly released her.

His lashes flickered. 'I didn't say I was.' He folded his arms, regarding her. 'But I have a strong urge to make love to you,' he said in a steady voice. 'And I'm fairly sure you wouldn't find it too repugnant to share my bed.'

'For life?' Her voice rose despite herself.

Zandro laughed. 'It's not a prison sentence,' he chided. More soberly, he added, 'I'll do my utmost to make you happy.' A deep glow lit his eyes now. 'You and Nicky. It won't be the first marriage to be entered on for reasons other than "true love." Marriages between people who hardly know each other apparently have as much chance of success as any other. Plenty of couples stay together for the sake of their children. Can't we come together for the same reason?'

He sounded so persuasive, so convincing. The kiss had been a devastating opening gambit. Now he was pulling out all the stops.

And he had the upper hand, including the higher moral ground. He didn't need to do this. The offer was, on the face of it, an extraordinarily generous gesture.

'Couldn't we be joint guardians?' she asked.

'It isn't the same, and I don't know if it's possible. The situation could be difficult if I married someone else. You want to be a permanent, everyday presence in Nicky's life, with the right to have a say in his up-bringing—well, this way you can.'

'I don't know.' She felt dazed, at sea. Maybe she was dreaming and would wake up soon.

If only the last year had been a dream, her sister alive, all this never having happened.

She knew she wasn't dreaming. In real life people died. And people made decisions, some good and some bad, and then did the best they could and muddled through somehow. They even got married for all the wrong reasons—and what were the wrong reasons, really? Lust? Greed? Pregnancy? Simple foolishness, mistaking infatuation for everlasting love?

All of those and more. And were any of them better than a marriage undertaken for the sake of a mother-less, fatherless child?

'Think of Nicky,' Zandro said, as though he'd read her thoughts. 'You insisted he needs a mother. I've thought of marrying simply to give him one.'

'You never met the right woman?'

He shrugged. 'If she seemed right for me she was wrong for Nicky.'

And he'd given them up for the child's sake? 'There must be a trail of disappointed women in your past.'

The skin at his eyes crinkled. 'One or two,' he al-lowed. 'It's been less than a year since I've had Nicky, and he took a good deal of my time before you came along.'

She hadn't known that either. Had he been holding back while she got to know her supposed son?

He said, 'I'll give you some time to decide. Perhaps we should go on a date.'

'A date?' She looked at him blankly.

'It's usual for…er…courting couples. We could see a show, have supper afterwards—just us two, away from here.'

'Are you *asking* me on a date?'

'I'm asking you. Say yes.'

Her turn to laugh, with a slight edge of incipient hysteria. How typical of him to make it sound like an order. 'Is that your standard way of asking a girl out?'

'It usually works.' He was poker-faced, but his eyes gave him away. He was baiting, expecting a comeback.

She couldn't think of one. 'I suppose,' she said, 'one date won't hurt.' In truth it would be nice to get out of the house, have an evening of entertainment. Making her voice very dry, she assured him, 'I'll look forward to it.'

He wore a tuxedo, and when she saw him in it as she came down the stairs, having put on a shot-silk-look synthetic dress in a topaz colour with go-anywhere medium-heeled shoes, she was immediately sure this evening was a mistake. Zandro looked so sexy, so assuredly male, and so confident. How was she going to get through several hours of his company without swooning at his feet?

Just looking at him made her entire limbs warm and fluid. She stumbled on the bottom stair and he was instantly at her side, his arm about her waist, briefly holding her close.

She inhaled the scent of his aftershave and the underlying unique aroma of his skin before he released her and placed a hand at her elbow, saying, 'Shall we go?'

His car was big and she was glad the leather seats were far enough apart to give her a chance to regain her equilibrium. He didn't talk much as he drove, merely inquiring if she was comfortable, if she'd like to listen to the radio or a CD, and remarking on the weather and the traffic conditions.

They'd chosen a musical show—Cara didn't feel ready to cope with drama and tragedy—and for minutes at a time she was able to forget her recent bereavement, the subsequent problems, and her present dilemma. But she was never able to wholly dismiss Zandro's presence at her side, his sleeve occasionally brushing against her arm, his black-clad thigh only inches from hers as he stretched his legs before him, his head sometimes turning in her direction to give her a long look. She tried not to look back, but couldn't resist a peek at his strong profile when he returned his attention to the stage.

Following the interval, when the lights dimmed, he reached for her hand and folded it into his. She stiffened her fingers, but after a moment let them relax, and he turned to give her a lazy smile. His thumb caressed her wrist, and she totally lost track of what was happening on stage, concentrating instead on controlling her breathing, trying to ignore the sensations that were consuming her entire body.

She'd never met a man like Zandro before, one who could thrill her whole being with a casual touch, engender heart-pounding desire with a look. Never been so powerfully drawn to someone that she could scarcely think straight. From the first, when she was convinced he was a heartless business tycoon whose family's foundation was ambition and pride rather than affection, she'd been conscious of that overpowering sexuality. And wary, afraid to admit her susceptibility.

He'd breached her defences with astonishing ease. And now he wanted to marry her.

Marriage to Zandro. Her breath caught, and her fingers within his fluttered. She felt the glance he cast her but didn't acknowledge it. He tightened his grip, and moved their joined hands to rest on his thigh, the back of hers against his trousers. Through the fabric she could feel the tautness of his skin, the hard muscle beneath. Silently she drew in a deep breath and let it out. The figures on stage were a blur of colour and action, the music drowned by the beat of her heart.

If merely holding the man's hand did this to her, what would it be like making love with him?

Like nothing she'd ever known.

Not a thought that helped. She gave a determined tug at her imprisoned hand, and Zandro turned to her again, releasing her. She kept her eyes fixed on the spectacle before them and tangled her fingers in her lap.

He folded his arms and settled back in his seat.

Outside, he took possession again of her hand. 'There's a restaurant not far from here where we can have coffee and something to eat,' he said. 'Are you okay to walk?'

'Yes, fine.' Her shoes were comfortable enough for a short walk.

In the restaurant the tables were laid with red cloths, and candles set in miniature floral wreaths. The background music was muted. She wondered if he'd chosen the place for its proximity to the theatre or its romantic decor. He seemed to be known to the maître d' and it crossed her mind that he'd brought other women here. That thought stabbed her with what she realised dismayingly was pure, green jealousy.

After they'd ordered, Zandro said, 'Tell me about yourself.'

Was that another of his gambits that 'usually worked'? 'You seem to know so much about me already,' she countered. 'Why don't *you* start?'

Slight surprise coloured his smile. 'Okay,' he agreed, after a pause. 'We haven't always lived where we are now. That's down to my father's hard work and enterprise. And my mother's support.'

He talked of a childhood that had few luxuries at first, living in a small house in Brisbane, shared with his mother's family, then a move to the suburbs as the business prospered. 'We came here when I was a teenager. My mother's sister had shifted here, and although it's only a train ride away, or an hour or so by road, my mother missed the closeness they were used to. The house was her dream home. My father had it built for her.'

'Were you close to your brother then?' Cara asked as their food arrived. He hadn't really told her much about himself, only the milieu that had surrounded him.

He looked down at his wineglass, one hand absently twirling the stem, his eyes hidden behind thick black lashes. 'I loved Rico very much, although there was an age gap so we didn't have a lot in common. My mother has always regretted she didn't have a daughter.' He glanced up. 'What about you? Was your childhood happy?'

'Very. My parents were sensible and loving. They laid down rules and made sure we followed them. We…I miss them a lot.'

'You must miss your sister too.' His eyes were fixed on her. 'Twins are extra close, aren't they?'

'Our parents encouraged us to be individuals.' Despite sharing many traits they'd always had distinct personalities—Lia the impulsive one, Cara steadier, more cautious, accustomed to extricating her sister from scrapes. Although only minutes older she'd always felt a responsibility to her more volatile twin. 'But Lia wanted to be…free of me.'

'Of you?' His gaze sharpened.

A familiar ache squeezed her heart, and she took some wine. 'She came to Australia on her own because she felt smothered.'

Lia had accused Cara of always holding her back, of being possessive and domineering. 'You're happy in your rut and you want me to stay in it with you, locked in the same little box. Just because we're twins you think you own me or something. Little Miss Perfect, never getting into trouble—Mummy and Daddy's little angel, and why couldn't I be more like you? Well, I'm *not* you—and I don't need you to tell me what I should or shouldn't do. Get your own life!' she'd stormed. 'And stop trying to live mine for me!' In hindsight, a prophetic phrase.

Cara had reeled under the onslaught. Possessive? Domineering? Was that how Lia saw Cara's steady, protective love for her more impulsive sister? Of course they'd patched it up with each other the next day, but the accusations had shaken Cara to the core, and remained in her mind like malevolent little thorns under the skin, hardly noticeable until some painful reminder made her guarded.

If it hadn't been for that bitter exchange when she'd glimpsed resentments she hadn't known her sister harboured, she would have heeded the always-present worry that had followed Lia's departure—would have initiated contact more often, and later taken a flight to Sydney to see for herself that her sister was doing all right.

It was still too painful to speak about. Cara forced

down a mouthful of food, past the lump in her throat. 'For a time she was happy here. She was madly in love with Rico.'

Quietly Zandro said, 'They weren't good for each other, Cara.'

At least he wasn't blaming Lia now. 'I suppose not,' she agreed huskily.

He placed a hand over hers where it lay on the red cloth. 'If I'm partly responsible for her death, I'm doing my best to atone for it.'

Withdrawing her hand from his, she said, 'Did you ask me to marry you to salve your conscience?' Knowing it wasn't fair to blame him, the words nevertheless sticking in her throat, she admitted, 'Lia was responsible for her own life.'

After a small pause he said, 'I want to marry you for a number of reasons. For Nicky's sake, of course. But also because my mother would like more grandchildren.' He looked up, a teasing grin curling a corner of his mouth. 'And not least because I want very much to take you to bed. Which my parents wouldn't countenance without a wedding ring.' He swallowed some pasta, sipped his wine again and regarded her over the rim of the glass. 'I hope you don't object to having children?'

She'd assumed she would one day. With the right man. Was it possible Zandro was that man? A fleeting mental picture entered her mind of three children, one with her green eyes and brown hair, the other two darker, like Zandro.

Quickly she picked up her glass and gulped down some wine, banishing the image. 'I like children,' she hedged.

'Good.' He went back to eating.

*   *   *

At the house when they returned the hallways were dimly lit, the rest of the place in darkness. Zandro escorted her to her bedroom door and pushed it open.

'Thank you,' she said. 'It was a nice evening.'

With laughter in his voice, he said, 'Then thank me properly, Cara.' His arms came about her and she put her hands on his sleeves, not protesting. When his mouth coaxed her lips apart she let her hands slide about his neck, her body arch against him, yielding to his touch, his kiss.

Everything about them whirled away in darkness. The only thing she knew was this meeting of lips, of breath, of tongues. After a while his lips left hers and he kissed her neck, her shoulder, then eased down the edge of her dress until it was low over her breast, and his lips pressed hotly to the soft flesh above her bra. Cara made a small sound and he laughed deep in his throat. She caught a flash of light in his eyes as he raised his head and kissed her again, in naked passion.

She answered it with a passion of her own, aroused beyond bearing, shaking with it, her legs scarcely able to hold her.

At last Zandro wrenched his mouth away, loosened his hold and caught her face between his hands, then placed another kiss on her lips, brief but searing. 'Cara,' he said, his voice thick and slow. 'You know what your name means in Italian?'

Darling. She nodded, unable to form any words.

She thought he smiled. In the muted light it was hard to tell. He moved his hands, trailing them down to her shoulders. One hand went to her back, the other taking a slow journey over her breasts, down to her stomach, then both palms shaped her hips and caressed her behind before he stepped back. 'Don't take too long making up your mind,' he said. 'Goodnight, *cara*.'

She stood watching him walk towards his room. Only when he reached it did she come to life and slip inside her own, closing the door and going unsteadily to the bed, to sit down with her arms wrapped about her. It was a wide bed, big enough for two, and she had a shockingly clear vision of herself and Zandro sharing it, making wild, abandoned love on the linen sheets. Her whole body was on fire. She needed a cold shower.

She settled for a lukewarm one, although she'd already showered earlier. As the water cascaded over her she recalled Zandro saying he'd heard her showering, and hastily turned the tap off. Straining her ears, she heard water running next door. Maybe he too was dousing the fires of desire. Stifling an urge to giggle, she stepped out and towelled herself briskly, determined to blot out a persistent image of Zandro standing under a shower, his marvellously sexy body bared, wet and gleaming.

Her sleep was troubled by erotic dreams from which she half woke every so often with a sense of disappointment that it was only a dream, to turn over and force herself to think of something else before drifting off again.

The next day was Sunday again, and she was grateful that the extended family came for their usual after-church visit. By evening she was able to face him over dinner almost as though the previous night's passionate interlude had never happened.

Summer was on its way, and the day had been hot and windless. Helping Mrs Walker and Mrs Brunellesci tidy up after the guests, Cara checked around the sitting room for missed toys or crockery, wiping a film of moisture from under her hairline.

'Feel like a swim?' Zandro asked.

She did, but hesitated to say so. Involuntarily her gaze shifted to the window, where the ocean showed blue and inviting. 'In the sea?' She had swum a few times in the pool at the back of the house, but knew that Zandro preferred surfing the breakers on the beach.

'Get changed,' he said. 'I'll see you in a few minutes.'

The suggestion of an order made her hackles stand on tiptoe, but it wasn't worth arguing, cutting off her own nose. She went upstairs and put on her swimsuit, and was winding a towel about her body when there was a tap on the door. Zandro called, 'Are you ready, Cara?'

'Coming.' She tucked in the towel and opened the door. He cast a swift glance over her, seeming to approve, then as they descended the stairs his arm went around her, his hand curving over her bare shoulder and remaining there all the way to the beach, until they paused to discard their towels and wade into the water.

'We'll stop swimming in the sea soon,' he said after surfacing beside her. 'In summer the locals tend to avoid it.'

'Because of jellyfish?'

'And other stinging sea creatures. The beach will be crowded with tourists anyway.'

She floated on her back, moving her hands lazily. 'Don't they get stung?'

'Sometimes, but it doesn't seem to put them off. It's pretty safe here. Bluebottle stings are fairly common—

painful but not fatal. The real nasties are mostly further north.'

He ducked under the water, swam beneath her and came up on the other side. Cara turned over and breast-stroked away from him, but he kept pace. A swell lifted them and let them down gently beyond the crest. Zandro was closer to her now. He dived again, seeming completely at home in the water. This time he surfaced just in front of her, and she stopped swimming, tread-ing water instead.

'Take a breath,' Zandro said. He came nearer, pull-ing her into an embrace as she sucked in some air. His mouth, cool and salty, closed on hers and they sank under the water into a soundless green world, their legs tangling together, slick skin against skin.

CHAPTER NINE

THE kiss lasted only seconds, until Zandro kicked upwards and they burst into the sunlit air and he let her go, his challenging, triumphant smile dazzling.

The erotic charge had been mind-blowing. Despite the cool water Cara's skin was hot. She swam away from him and felt his hand circle her ankle, drawing her back, and he was beside her again. 'What's the hurry?' he asked, releasing her.

'I came out here to swim.'

'That's what we're doing.'

She glared at him—as best she could while her foolish body yearned mortifyingly for his touch—tossed wet hair from her eyes and changed her stroke to an over-arm crawl. Zandro laughed again and this time he didn't follow.

Later, Cara was ready to get into bed when she heard footsteps along the passageway outside. They stopped outside her door and she held her breath. Then they went on, and moments later she heard Zandro's bedroom door close.

She caught herself in the full-length mirror on the door of the big wardrobe, her pose frozen, her face showing apprehension and longing. Her nightshirt was shapeless and opaque, a slightly faded pink. She recalled Zandro looking at it with laughter in his eyes.

Perhaps she should buy something glamorous, filmy—sexy. If she were to marry Zandro…

If…?

She lifted a photo from the bedside table, where she'd placed it after Zandro blew her cover. Climbing into bed, she studied the picture of two smiling girls, taken when she and Lia were eighteen, her favourite of them together. 'What should I do, Lia?' she murmured. In Lia's eyes Zandro was an opportunistic, manipulative child-snatcher who had helped drive his brother from the family home. And yet Rico had named his baby for his father and Lia had agreed to Zandro's guardianship.

Sighing, Cara put aside the photo and turned out the bedside light, to lie awake for hours staring into the darkness, her mind going round in ever-decreasing circles.

Next evening, taking over from Barbara, Cara bathed Nicky and dressed him in his pyjamas before taking him downstairs to say goodnight to the others.

Lately Nicky was trying to walk, latching on to any adult willing to hold his hands and walk behind him while he practised this interesting new skill. Now he insisted on negotiating the stairs with Cara's help, hanging on to her hand with one of his pudgy little ones while the other clutched at each successive banister in turn. One step at a time, it was a laborious process. They were halfway down when the front door opened and Zandro appeared. He must have worked late because he was still wearing his office suit and tie.

Nicky let out an excited cry of 'Dee-dee!' and missed a step, unbalancing Cara as she swooped to catch him and ended up plonked on the stair with him safe in her arms.

Zandro bounded up the staircase three at a time and crouched just below her. 'Are you okay?'

'Yes.' And so was Nicky, stretching out his arms to his uncle, a huge grin on his face.

Zandro took him, giving him a stern look. 'What were you trying to do to your auntie, young man?'

Nicky laughed and jiggled in the strong arms that held him, grabbed a handful of black hair and cooed, 'Dee-ee.'

'That's all very well—' Zandro planted a kiss on the baby's plump cheek '—you little monster.'

'Monna,' Nicky echoed with great satisfaction, giggled again and burrowed his head against the man's shoulder. Zandro laid his hand over the downy curls, looking down with a smile.

The picture they made hit Cara with stunning force. Zandro might not be perfect, but his love for his nephew was deep and genuine. She could no longer doubt it. Or Nicky's for him and Mrs Brunellesci— even for his grandfather.

How could she ever have thought of taking Nicky away from these people who loved him so much? Conscience-smitten, she bit her lip.

'Zandro,' she said quietly, and waited until he looked up at her. Her own gaze dropped to the child in his arms. Somehow that made it easier, assured her she was doing the right thing. 'I've decided. I will marry you.'

For a moment everything seemed to be frozen in time. She heard her own words echo on the air. Had she really said them? Entered into a frightening commitment, altered the course of her life?

His hand left Nicky's hair and reached out to her. A thumb stroked her cheek, and his fingers curled about the back of her head as he leaned towards her, bringing her close enough for him to press a lingering kiss on her mouth. 'I swear I'll make sure you won't regret it,' he said. '*Cara mia.*'

Nicky wriggled, until Zandro drew away to steady him. Still holding the baby, he made to pass him over as Cara got to her feet.

Nicky shook his head, clinging to his uncle.

Zandro laughed. 'All right,' he said, turning to head down the stairs, and taking Cara's hand. 'We have some news for your Nonna and Nonno.' He led her into the big front room where his parents waited, Mrs Brunellesci with some of her handiwork, Domenico reading a business magazine.

'Papa, Mamma,' he said, 'I have something to tell you. Cara has consented to be my wife…and Nicky's new mother.'

For long seconds neither of them reacted. Cara thought it might have been better if Zandro had broken it to them in private. Her heart sank. If they disapproved—and they must be aware that this was hardly a whirlwind love match, so wouldn't they be concerned for their son?—there could be major problems ahead.

Zandro said gently, 'Congratulations are in order.'

Mrs Brunellesci finally lifted her hands as if to extend them, then looked at her husband, who rose slowly from his chair, steadied himself on his stick and approached his son, offering his hand.

Zandro took it, and his father kissed him on both cheeks, growling, '*Complimenti,* my son.'

He turned to Cara a fierce look, his eyes boring into hers. 'I welcome my son's bride,' he said, and brushed dry lips over one cheek, then the other.

Mrs Brunellesci had risen too, seeming uncertain but pleased. When her husband stepped back she opened her arms and gave Cara a warm, enveloping hug. 'This is good,' she said, and reached up to take Zandro's face between her hands, pulling him down for a kiss. 'I told you, it's time you got married.'

Returning to Cara, she added, 'And you won't take away our Nico.' Her mouth trembled and she wiped away a tear. 'Zandro said it was impossible, but...I am frightened, very much.'

'I'm so sorry.' Mrs Brunellesci had been kind to her despite her fear. 'But I'd promised my sister...'

'*Si*, I understand. But now we are all happy. All one family!'

Cara had no time for doubts or regrets. The cousins and aunt were astonished and excited, and everyone seemed to expect to have a hand in preparing for the wedding. Two little girls begged to be bridal attendants and Cara said weakly, 'Of course, but it isn't going to be a big wedding...'

She turned to Zandro, panic in her eyes, and he told his relatives, 'It's not so long since Cara's sister died, so a lavish wedding wouldn't be appropriate. It will just be family and a few friends.'

She was grateful, though Mrs Brunellesci's disappointed face gave her a pang. Later, as she and Zandro walked together on the beach, recovering from the effusive congratulations and enthusiastic suggestions of his family, she said, 'I think your mother wanted to see you tie the knot in style, a wedding with all the trimmings.'

'Is that what *you* want?' he asked.

'No! But...I don't like to cheat her out of something she's been looking forward to. She won't have another chance.'

He stopped, taking her hands in his. 'My mother

wants to see me happy, that's the only important thing to her.'

'She must know this isn't a love match!'

He glanced up at the sky, where a lone seagull was calling in rather melancholy fashion, then looked back at Cara. 'She hardly knew my father when they married. Their families introduced them just before he emigrated—he was on the lookout for a wife, and she was suitable. They corresponded for a year, and then she came out to join him. Her sister followed later. Mamma lived in a convent hostel until she and Papa married, which they did as soon as they could. There were strict rules about having men in the place, or staying out after ten. So they used to sit in the hostel parlour with other people all around, trying to get to know each other.'

'They seem happy. Although your father is a bit…'

Zandro laughed. 'He's an autocrat. But he adores Mamma, and when she puts her mind to it she can get him to do anything she wants. Anything she thinks is right.'

'I have a feeling,' she said with a direct look, 'you take after your father.'

'And I have a feeling you won't stand for it if I become too much like him.'

'I won't let you order me about,' she warned. 'And I'll stand up for Nicky.'

He smiled, apparently unconcerned. 'If you feel the need, you should. I hope we can work out most differences by talking them through.' He lifted her hands and kissed them, one by one. Then he drew her into his arms. 'Or in more interesting ways,' he said, before he kissed her with an erotic intensity that sent her senses into overdrive and blanked out thought entirely.

* * *

Mrs Brunellesci and her sister insisted that even though the wedding was low-key, Cara must have a special dress. They took her into Brisbane, and spent a highly enjoyable day with her as their mannequin, dragging her to several bridal boutiques before everyone agreed on the perfect dress.

It was white—they insisted nothing else would do for a bride—and to her relief simply cut, with flowing, delicate lace sleeves that just brushed her elbows, and a discreet trim of tiny seed pearls about the neckline and the ankle-length hem.

She hadn't intended to wear a veil, but when Mrs Brunellesci shyly produced the lovely lace-edged circle she'd worn for her own wedding and asked anxiously if Cara liked it, she didn't have the heart to turn it down.

Zandro had presented her with a diamond engagement ring, one large stone with two smaller ones set in a slender gold circle. 'We'll change it if you don't like it,' he said.

She did like it, and was glad she hadn't been asked to help choose it. That would have seemed something of a farce.

Zandro acted as if they were any normal engaged couple, taking her out, introducing her to his friends—most of whom, to her relief, she liked—and touching her a lot. An arm about her waist or shoulders, his fingers entwined in hers. She was almost ashamed of the sensations he aroused with the lightest skimming of his fingers over her skin.

And he kissed her at her bedroom door each night—possessive, arousing kisses that left her unsatisfied and disturbed.

They had pre-marriage counselling with the priest

who was to conduct the service, emphasising the serious nature of what they were undertaking. Even if it had been in her nature, she couldn't pretend she hadn't gone into this with open eyes. Australian law, and the church, didn't allow over-hasty weddings.

Cara had invited a few close friends, but only two could make it on the day, although Zandro had offered to pay the fares for anyone she specially wanted. She had no adult attendants, but Zandro's cousin's little girls solemnly preceded her down the aisle. Suddenly missing her sister's presence at her wedding, she blinked away a tear as she approached the altar, and Zandro turned to face her.

He looked almost stern, his eyes homing in on the tear, and she smiled to banish it. A wavering smile that he didn't return, only reaching for her hand as she passed her small bouquet to one of the flower girls before both went to sit mouselike throughout the remainder of the ceremony.

She gave her responses quietly but her voice was quite steady, the warmth and strength of Zandro's hand clasping hers giving her courage.

Afterwards they went back to the house, all the guests joining them for a catered buffet wedding breakfast. The rooms had been decorated for the occasion with white ribbons, silver bells and flowers, and tiny caskets of sweets were handed out to the guests as mementoes. If it wasn't a big wedding there were enough cousins and friends to have a party, and the family was going to mark the occasion in appropriate fashion.

The celebration was still going on when Zandro and Cara left in his car to drive to Brisbane. Zandro had suggested a honeymoon in the tropical north, or on a Pacific island, perhaps a short cruise. She'd turned all of them down, not wanting to leave Nicky for long. 'He's still getting to know me and I don't want him to forget me. Do we need to go away?'

'I refuse to spend my wedding night in my parents' house,' Zandro had said, so they'd settled for a night in one of Brisbane's top hotels, and then a flight to Auckland where she could arrange to rent her house out and remove anything she wanted.

'I have to do that sometime,' Cara had pointed out. 'I know it's not a normal honeymoon, but then…this isn't a normal marriage.'

'All right,' Zandro agreed finally, giving her a cool, thoughtful look. 'Later we'll have a proper holiday.'

When they were ushered into a suite on the fifteenth floor Cara nearly choked. The bed seemed enormous, dominating the room even though that was twice the size of any hotel room she'd seen before, and there was marble and gilt everywhere, even a couple of cherubs holding up a swathe of white tulle over the gilded bed head. When she took off her shoes her toes were buried in the thick pile of the carpet. A hugely ornate oval mirror featuring a riot of gold-painted roses and ribbons was on one wall, while a chaise longue covered in deep red velvet stood against another. The bathroom door was open, revealing more marble, two washbasins shaped like giant scallop shells, and gold faucets. 'Heavens!' she said faintly.

Zandro closed the door after the bellboy and came to her side. 'A bit over the top,' he agreed, his mouth curving as he moved his gaze to the glass table flanked by chairs that were pretending to have come from sixteenth-century France. On the table were two crystal flutes and a silver bucket of ice holding a bottle of champagne. Zandro moved towards it. 'If I'm going to sleep in this room I need some of that. How about you?'

She laughed, breaking the tension that had been building on the journey. Zandro had tried to make conversation, asking about her friends who had flown over, commenting on the food at the reception, gently mocking his mother who had been in a last-minute panic about everything, and his father who had done his best to keep out of the way ever since the preparations began. She knew her replies had been stilted, betraying an increasing, ridiculous nervousness.

He handed her a champagne flute and touched his own to it. 'To us, Cara…and our future.'

There was a sliding door to a balcony outside. Zandro opened it and they stepped out, standing side by side looking over the lights of the city, the black areas showing where the river ran through it. A little breeze sprang up, and Cara shivered.

Zandro said, 'Are you cold?'

'Not really.' She finished her drink. 'I'll have a shower.'

He stayed where he was until she came out of the bathroom, wearing a nightgown of rich gold satin with a cream lace bodice held by shoestring straps.

'Very nice,' he said, stopping in the doorway, still holding his champagne flute. 'I don't wear pyjamas. Do you mind?'

Cara shook her head. He slanted her a smile and closed the door. Then he put his glass back on the table and drew the curtains across. 'We'd hardly be overlooked this far up,' he said, 'but I guess there could be voyeurs out there.'

He snapped open his suitcase, then took out a toilet bag and strolled to the bathroom. 'I won't be long.'

He wasn't, coming back with a towel tucked about his waist. She'd turned out all the lights except the one on the side of the bed she'd left for him, and was sitting with her knees up under the covers, flipping through a magazine provided by the hotel, without taking in any of it.

'Do you want the light on or off?' Zandro asked.

'Off.' She closed the magazine, but clutched it between her fingers.

Zandro flicked the switch and the room was black. He said, 'Then I'd like to open the curtains, if that's okay. No one will be able to see now, and a little light would be…useful. I'd like to be able to see my bride.'

A shiver of mingled apprehension and excitement ran over her skin. 'Okay.' She carefully placed the magazine on the night table as the curtains swished back and she saw Zandro silhouetted against the glow of the city lights, a high moon hanging motionless and pearl-white above them.

He came back to the bed, but instead of sliding into it sat down at her side. 'Are you tired?' he said. 'It's been quite a day.'

'Are you?' she countered.

He laughed softly. 'Not too tired to make love to you.' He touched her cheek very lightly, brushing back a strand of hair, then his fingers trailed down her neck, settled on her shoulder, toying with the thin strap that held her gown. 'But you seem a bit stressed.'

'A bit,' she admitted.

'If you want to wait—' his hand trailed down her arm, turning her blood to liquid fire '—you only need to say so.' He took her hand in his. 'When I do make love to you I want you to be awake and aware and enjoying every second.' He lifted the hand he held and kissed it—not on the back, but on her palm, cupping it while he pressed his mouth against her skin and dipped his tongue into the hollow. She could feel that he was freshly shaved, and the familiar scent of his aftershave teased her nostrils.

He raised his head, and she said, 'I'm awake now.' She was, every nerve end tingling with awareness, with anticipation.

Again he kissed her hand, then moved his lips to her wrist, sending a delicious thrill all the way to her toes. 'I'm glad of that,' he said. 'Thank you, Cara.'

He leaned over to kiss her shoulder, began tugging down the strap. 'Did I tell you what a beautiful bride you made?'

'No.' She murmured the word, hardly above a whisper, her whole being concentrating on what he was doing with his mouth, his hands, as he gently eased her against the pillows. Moonlight turned the bed sheets silver-blue.

Cool air laved her breasts when he slipped the satin down and bared them to the moonlight. His hands warmed them, stroking, cupping, bringing the dusky centres exquisitely to life.

Then he bent his head and hot waves of sensation coursed through her while he tasted, teased, wringing an inarticulate cry of sheer dizzying delight from her lips.

He lifted his mouth from her, smothered the cry with his own lips and kissed her deeply, pushing aside the covers between them. His hands shoved the nightgown down to her hips, soon sliding the garment away over her feet, and he was kissing her instep, her ankle, turning her to reach the tender skin at the back of her knee, the curve of her behind, the small of her back before allowing her to lie flat.

He made love to her as if he were adoring her body, learning it with exquisite care, teaching her to know his.

Now he was poised over her, the towel discarded. He touched a finger to her lips, and the indentation at the base of her throat, trailed a light touch down her body, stopping en route to tantalise and explore, until he reached the soft, secret folds between her legs. She gave a long, sobbing sigh and let her thighs open, and he said, on a note of tenderness she'd never heard from him before, 'Now, Cara?'

'Yes,' she whispered. Her arms came about his neck and she felt his weight, the breath heaving into his lungs, and then the satisfying, hard glide of his entry, filling her, stretching her, giving her such pleasure she thought she'd faint with it, the room swirling in blackness, the bed seeming to disappear, and she was floating on a sea of sensation, with Zandro's mouth on hers drinking in her cries of ecstasy, his arms holding her so close she could feel every inch of his masculine body in the throes of his own climax, their bodies no longer individual entities, but joined as one.

The words that had been used during the service today, she recalled hazily, drifting back to earth with her head against his shoulder, his arms still wound tightly about her. This was what they meant…*the two shall be one flesh*.

When they finally separated she felt empty and bereft. But within seconds Zandro was scooping her into his arms again. He kissed her mouth. 'I meant to be more patient. Was I too fast for you?'

He hadn't needed to be patient. Over the last month

he'd been building her up to a pitch of desire that needed release. 'No,' she said, and yawned against his skin.

She felt his body shake with silent laughter. 'Bored already?'

'Tired,' she corrected. 'But it's a nice tiredness. Thank you, Zandro. I was nervous,' she confessed, sheepishly.

'I know. Thank *you, cara,* for trusting me. Now go to sleep, while I practise being patient…at least until morning.'

At the airport Zandro bought Cara an opal pendant, full of dark fire. She was wearing it when, after booking into a hotel in Auckland, they went to her home, and once she'd unlocked the front door and opened it he said, 'I think this is my cue.'

He picked her up and carried her inside, then kissed her, let her down to her feet, and kissed her again, long and slow and sexy.

'Is there a bed in this house?' he asked.

More than one, but the room Cara had shared with Lia held too many memories, and they hadn't got around to getting rid of the big double bed her parents had slept in which still seemed to be theirs.

There were too many ghosts in this house. She'd thought about that when she opted for spending the nights with Zandro in a hotel. But Zandro was caressing her, his hands weaving magic, and she wanted him, reached up to return his kiss, lose herself in him. They were soon entwined on the sofa in the sitting room, in silent, breathless communion.

Then she showed him the other rooms, told him about a childhood spent in this house, and playing in the backyard where a willow tree still dangled the remnant of a rope that had held a swing her father made. She wept a little, and he held her, then took her back to the hotel and made her laugh over dinner, then took her to bed and with exquisite concentration on her needs gave her unmatched pleasure, taking his own only after making sure she was totally satisfied.

They found an agent who promised to get her good tenants. And then she packed some clothes and trinkets, a few books and mementoes. Having planned a disappearing act as soon as she returned to New Zealand, she had already stripped the house of anything extraneous to a new life with Nicky and stowed a lot of things into boxes. Some of the boxes went to charity shops and others were shipped to Australia for her.

The three days were busy, but sometimes she and Zandro swam in the hotel pool or strolled by the waterfront and ate at one of the cafes there, and at night, in the morning, before dinner—any time they could snatch—they made love…or, as Cara reminded herself, had wonderful, energetic, adventurous sex.

Because this wasn't love. They had married for other reasons entirely, and although the sex was more fantastic than she'd ever imagined sex could be, it was a physical release, not an emotional experience.

Occasionally during the day she caught a look in Zandro's eyes that was different from the glitter of desire, a look that held something else, perhaps respect, or surprise. She knew she had pleased him with her sexuality. He frankly delighted in the uninhibited responses that he aroused in her, arousing him in turn to further sensual heights, until they were both exhausted, panting in each other's arms.

When they'd taken the return flight and were back

at the Brunellesci mansion, Cara found that all her things had been shifted to Zandro's room.

'My mother takes it for granted,' Zandro said, 'that a married couple will share their room…and bed.'

'Of course,' she said, taking off her shoulder bag and placing it on the stool at his dressing table. It was a masculine room, with lots of maroon colouring and wood. The bed, a big one featuring a plain varnished headboard, had a maroon brocade cover fringed with heavy gold tassels.

'You can redecorate it if you like,' Zandro said. 'However you want.'

'With cupids,' she suggested, 'and a tulle swag?'

He laughed. 'I might put my foot down at that.' His arms came about her from behind, pulling her against him. He kissed the smooth skin just below her ear. 'Dinner won't be for another half an hour.' They had already seen and made a fuss of Nicky, who'd seemed pleased to have them back, before Barbara bore him off for his bath.

'Your parents will expect us downstairs. And Barbara will be bringing Nicky in.'

He turned her and kissed her on the mouth, making it long and deep. Then he held her a few inches away, smiling at her. 'You're right,' he said. 'Already bringing me into line. Am I going to be a henpecked husband?'

She gave him an ironic look. 'I hardly think that's likely.' As if he'd ever allow it.

Zandro laughed. She pulled away from him and he reluctantly released his hold.

She unpacked quickly, putting her things away in unfamiliar drawers and cupboards. There'd be more to come when the boxes arrived from New Zealand. She sighed, thinking of the empty house of her childhood, soon to be occupied by strangers, and closed a drawer.

Zandro was lounging on the bed watching her, his hands behind his head. Slightly rattled, she said, 'I hope you don't think I'm going to unpack for you! Because I can tell you, it isn't going to happen.' She bent over to reach a bottom drawer.

'The thought hadn't crossed my mind,' he said lazily. 'It can wait. Right now I'm enjoying the view.'

Cara straightened and swung around, to meet a frankly lascivious gaze. Colour rising to her cheeks, she said, 'Stop that!'

'I'm not doing anything,' he pointed out. His mouth curved and the skin about his eyes crinkled.

'The way you're looking at me...'

'Just looking. Is that a sin? We're married, remember? Of course, you're free to look at me the same way.'

She wondered if that was how she looked at him when he didn't know it. This level of desire was something new to her. She wanted Zandro with an intense hunger that she'd never expected, and that giving in to only assuaged for a short time. It was bewildering, rather bothersome, to feel she was a slave to uncontrollable passion. Especially when she and Zandro were in reality practically strangers. No matter what he'd said when he asked her to marry him, and how much time they'd spent together since, they still had a great deal about each other to learn.

'I'll go and see if Nicky's finished his bath,' she said, 'and take him down.'

'Sure.' Zandro swung his feet to the floor. 'See you later.'

*   *   *

Cara loved caring for Nicky, playing with him, watching him learn new things each day, helping him walk, coaching him in a new word. Even changing him while he gurgled playfully at her as if he'd made a smelly mess just to tease her. When he had a bout of fever she nursed him with Barbara's help, and during the painful emergence of another tooth she got up in the night to walk the floor with him, sending Barbara back to bed.

As she held him one evening, wrapped in a towel after his bath, Barbara said ruefully, 'I can see I'm going to be redundant before long.'

'Oh, I'm sorry, Barbara! But I suppose you're right.'

Zandro looked in the doorway, as he sometimes did before going downstairs, just to say hello to the baby. 'What was that?' he asked, taking the hand that Nicky held out to him.

Barbara told him, 'Just that Cara won't be needing me for much longer. I guess I'd better start thinking about looking for another job.'

Cara smiled at her, but Zandro's brows had drawn together.

He said, 'I'm sure we'll need you for some time yet, Barbara.'

'Well...' She looked from him to Cara. 'I'd miss Nicky, but it's up to you two, of course. I'll tidy up here if you want to put Nicky into his pyjamas, Cara.'

Cara carried Nicky to his room, and Zandro followed. 'What was that about?' he asked.

Surprised at his curt tone, she was jerked out of her absorption with the baby, turning to face Zandro. 'What?'

He was regarding her impatiently, looking formidable and immovable, much as he had when she'd first arrived at his doorstep. Her heart sank. Something told her that the honeymoon was over, the tender, considerate lover subsumed in the man of steely purpose. Zandro was back to being the man she'd met months before, who would let no woman bend him to her will, would brook no opposition and always won his battles.

CHAPTER TEN

'YOU told Barbara we don't need her?' Zandro demanded.

'Not exactly, but we won't. I can do everything she does for him.'

'You've come to this decision, without consulting me?'

Nonplussed, she said, 'It doesn't really affect you. Except that I come cheaper.'

Her attempt at humour failed. His expression if anything became more thunderous, and she was relieved that Nicky demanded her attention, giving her an excuse to turn away from Zandro.

He said to her back, 'I didn't marry you to turn you into a nursemaid!'

Nicky wriggled, and she put him down on the changing table, reaching for a nappy. 'No,' she said, 'you did it to turn me into a mother for Nicky. And mothers look after their children.'

'I told you that isn't the only reason. You're not only a mother, you're a wife.'

She fastened the nappy and hitched pyjamas over Nicky's freshly padded bottom, then guided an arm into a sleeve. He grinned at her, showing another new tooth just peeking through, and she tickled his tummy, making him giggle. 'Most mothers are,' she said. The other arm went into a sleeve and she started doing up snaps.

'We can afford to keep a nanny on.'

She picked up the baby and turned to face Zandro. 'I want to care for Nicky myself, it's what I promised.'

'Do you ever think about anything but Nicky and your damned promise to your sister?' There was suppressed violence in his tone, shocking her.

'I don't understand why you're so angry! What is this about?'

'It's about the fact that we're married,' he said. 'Husband and wife. There are certain expectations—'

His evident temper stirred her own, along with a bewildered unease. 'Are you complaining? I thought I'd fulfilled my marital duties quite adequately. Of course, if you expect me to be available every minute of the day—'

Zandro reached behind him and slammed the open door shut. 'I'm not talking about sex.'

'Then I have no idea what you mean.'

'Married couples do things together—go out, spend time with each other.'

'We do that.'

He flung a hand briefly out. 'With Nicky—family and friend things.'

'Yes—' She'd been accepted readily into the Brunellesci clan, and getting to know them all, seeing how Nicky was loved, warmed her heart.

Zandro didn't let her finish. 'I'd like to take my wife when I have to attend a society dinner or entertain visiting business contacts.'

After twice attending business functions she'd made either Nicky's needs or her own tiredness an excuse to avoid them. Dealing with a lively toddler was more exhausting than she'd expected. 'You want a corporate wife?' She remembered what Lia had said about Zandro's fanatical dedication to the family firm.

He came closer to her. Nicky, who had been looking from one to the other of them with wide eyes, stretched out his arms.

Zandro took him, his gaze still fixed on Cara. 'I want you to be a *wife*. My partner, not just a bed mate— great though that is.' A familiar glint lit his eyes, and as always her body responded, sending a shiver of desire from head to toe. 'Lately, every time I suggest something that doesn't include Nicky you've turned it down. You're with him every second of the day. And if I suggest an evening out—just the two of us—you're too tired. Even too tired, sometimes, to make love.'

She bit her lip, because that was true, although if she'd pleaded fatigue when Zandro drew her into his arms he'd simply held her until she drifted off to sleep.

He said in a tone that expected no comeback, 'I won't have you run ragged as my mother was when my brother and I were young. Barbara stays.'

His last word on the subject apparently. Cara fumed, formulating a cutting retort about autocrats and *What happened to working out our differences by discussion?* while Nicky, who had been examining Zandro's tie, pulled it free and put the end into his mouth. Zandro looked down and tugged the tie away, and Nicky's loud objection made further conversation impossible.

Cara picked up his favourite toy rabbit and handed it to him, but he batted it away to land on the floor.

There was a tapping at the door and Barbara entered. 'I'll take him,' she offered, expertly removing the baby from Zandro's arms. Nicky struggled furiously but the nanny held him firmly, talking to him and rubbing his back. She took a colourful clown toy down from a shelf and wiggled it in front of his eyes until the tantrum subsided and he reached for the toy.

'I'm going to get changed,' Zandro said. Looking at Cara, he added critically, 'You look as though you need a change too.' Nicky's bath time had been particularly energetic, and her blouse and skirt had large wet patches.

He waited at the door for her to precede him to their room, where he stripped and went into the bathroom. When he emerged Cara had put on a fresh dress and was brushing her hair in front of the big dressing table. In heavy silence she watched in the mirror as he crossed the room and took casual pants and a shirt from his wardrobe. He had a magnificent body. Just looking at him made her veins throb with anticipation of their lovemaking later.

Zandro pulled on the pants, turning as he closed the zip. His eyes met hers in the mirror and he paused. He was still looking grim, but she saw the desire flicker into his eyes, the faint movement of a muscle in his cheek.

Cara looked away, took a final sweep over her hair and shook it back, briefly closing her eyes.

Zandro's hand plucked the brush from her fingers and put it on the dressing table. She raised her eyes to see his reflection right behind hers, his chest bare, his face taut, dark eyes glittering.

He turned her with his hands on her shoulders, then his mouth was on hers, seeking, demanding, taking and giving at the same time, with an edge of some primitive emotion—a vestige of his earlier anger. Her heart pounded and her whole body was instantly suffused with longing. His tongue plunged into her mouth and she took it eagerly, pressing herself against the hard bulge of his erection.

His hands were under skirt, stripping away her flimsy panties. She ran her own hands down his back, exploring skin and muscle, the groove of his spine, then slipped her fingers into the waistband of his trousers. He hadn't done up the snap, and she found the zip and pulled it down. His trousers fell and he kicked them away, pulled off his underpants and returned to her, naked, big, and so sexy she could have wept.

Reaching behind her, he swept aside the hairbrush, a comb and a bottle of perfume on the dressing table, and hitched her onto it. He lifted his head and she realised he was looking at their reflection in the mirror.

She raised her hands to his face and brought his head down for another kiss, and he willingly complied. His hands were under her thighs, coaxing them apart, and then he edged her forward a little and thrust into her while she clung to him, her arms about his neck as if she were drowning and he her saviour, her head back. Her lips parted on a long moan and almost instantly she climaxed with wave after wave of ecstasy.

His hands were in her hair, holding her as his mouth crashed down again on hers, open and hungry. And she heard the guttural sound of satisfaction he made in his throat when he followed her into the bright, swirling storm-centre of passion.

While it subsided, the tiny aftershocks fading away, he still held her, her forehead resting on his shoulder, which was damp with a film of sweat. 'You are beautiful,' he said, his voice muffled by her hair.

'So are you,' Cara returned dreamily. She still felt floaty, not quite returned to the real world.

Zandro laughed, and she felt it through her body.

She'd thought she was spent, but desire stirred again, and she moved against him.

He sucked in a breath, and responded instantly. 'Are you comfortable here?' he asked in her ear.

'Yes.' More than comfortable. Passion was building anew.

His hands fumbled behind her and drew down the zip of her dress, and she lifted her arms to help him get the garment off. Zandro unclipped her bra and disposed of that too, so she was as naked as he.

His arms went around her, and her breasts pressed against his chest. He gave a low 'Ah!' of pleasure, and she pushed back slightly against his hold, moving the hardened tips across his skin.

'Tease,' he growled, shifting one hand to capture a tight dark pink bud between a thumb and forefinger, his palm cupping the soft flesh surrounding it.

'You too,' she whispered as he in turn teased, a gentle torture. She nipped his earlobe and he grabbed her chin, tilted her face and kissed her with deep, erotic thoroughness.

The ultimate satisfaction came, slower, and different, as every time was different, unique. But just as breathtaking as their lovemaking always was.

Afterwards they took a quick shower together and then hastily dressed again and went down decorously to dinner.

No more was said about Barbara. Cara made an effort to accept when Zandro suggested they have a night out, alone or with his friends. She accompanied him to business engagements and social functions and as she gradually learned something of how his world functioned outside of home, she began asking questions and finding the answers fascinating. He was held in high regard by his colleagues, and Cara discovered she could enjoy a business dinner or a reception for some visiting dignitary. Apparently the Brunellesci empire was important enough for Zandro to be asked sometimes to take part in consultations with government committees.

Most of her day was still spent with Nicky, who was walking by himself now, and regularly falling over his own feet in his eagerness to explore his expanding world, where so many more things were newly within his reach. Mrs Brunellesci—Mamma, she urged Cara to call her now—and the housekeeper had reorganised the sitting room, sweeping the low tables clean of precious ornaments, and gates had been installed at the stairs.

Cara never pleaded tiredness again when in the privacy of their bedroom Zandro reached for her. She knew his skilful lovemaking would bring the response he wanted, even if at first she was slow to react.

But one night she failed to hide her initial lethargy and he stilled his caresses, a heavy hand on her breast. 'You don't want to do this, do you?' he asked.

She began to answer, but was overtaken by a yawn, stifling it with her hand. 'I'm sorry,' she mumbled.

He moved away a few inches. 'You've been looking more tired than usual lately,' he said. 'Barbara says you've pretty much taken over from her.' Irritably he asked, 'Why don't you let the woman do her job?'

'It's my job! I'm his mother.'

'We're back to that again,' he said wearily. 'What the hell is the matter with you, that you can't trust anyone else to care for him?'

'Nicky's a baby,' she said. 'Someone has to watch him every moment.'

'The someone doesn't always have to be you. You said your sister felt smothered—has it occurred to you that Nicky might one day feel the same?'

She went very still, her heart going cold inside her. Her head turned on the pillow so he couldn't see her face, and she swallowed hard.

Zandro touched her shoulder. 'I don't mean to hurt you, but you can't make up to Nicky for failing to save his mother by martyring yourself to him instead, Cara. In time he too will need his independence. And what will you have then?'

She couldn't speak, wanting to tell him he was wrong, but a knot of dread sat in her stomach. A faint nausea that had troubled her at dinner, leading her to pick at her food and leave half of it uneaten, returned with force. She sat up, her forehead cold, and slipped out of bed, heading for the bathroom and closing the door.

After a very uncomfortable five minutes she was rinsing her face and mouth at the basin when Zandro called, 'Cara? Are you all right?'

She wiped her face on a towel and opened the door. He was standing there, waiting.

'You're as white as a sheet,' he said, even as she reached to flick off the bathroom light.

Without consulting her he picked her up in his arms and carried her to the bed. 'Shall I call a doctor? Why didn't you say something!'

'It comes and goes,' she said as he lowered her onto the mattress and sat beside her. 'I don't need a doctor. Not yet. You said you'd like other children—well…'

Zandro was still and silent. She couldn't see his face

in the darkness of the room. Then he said in an oddly hoarse voice, 'You're pregnant?'

'I'm not sure yet, but the symptoms seem to fit.'

He insisted on her seeing a doctor, and on coming with her. Afterwards he reminded her, 'You need plenty of rest.'

'The doctor also said to get regular exercise,' Cara reminded him.

'I don't think lifting a hefty toddler and running 'round after him is what she had in mind.'

'It's all the exercise a lot of pregnant women get,' Cara retorted. 'None of my friends with young families can afford a full-time nanny.' Although one or two of them had told her ruefully that sex had become simply an extra chore.

'We can. My mother miscarried a little girl when my brother and I were young—she still grieves for that baby. I would never forgive myself if the same thing happened to you—to our child.'

Truthfully, she was grateful that Barbara was there to allow her to take a nap when the fatigue that Zandro's mother told her was a common part of pregnancy overtook her.

Zandro imposed constraints on their lovemaking, at first abstaining altogether, and even after being assured by the doctor that intercourse would do the baby no harm, treating Cara with such care she might have been made of glass. He watched her every minute he was home, insisting on her lying down if she was pale, worrying if she didn't feel like eating, and enlisting his mother and Barbara to help him make her take things easy.

One Sunday after the family left he followed her

upstairs where she'd used the bathroom and was taking a minute to tidy her hair in front of the dressing table. He tried to persuade her to have a nap before dinner, and she snapped at him, 'Oh, do stop fussing, Zandro! Pregnancy isn't an illness. I'm a perfectly healthy grown woman, and I can decide for myself if I need a rest or how much food I should eat.'

'You're the mother of my unborn child,' he said stubbornly. 'It's my duty to look after you both.'

Something chilled her. Duty was why he had taken on Nicky's care, the primary reason he had married her.

Zandro enjoyed sex with her, he'd made that very clear. But he had probably enjoyed the same pleasure with other women before his marriage. Perhaps even greater enjoyment, with partners more experienced than Cara.

Long before Cara's arrival in Australia he'd grown to love Nicky. He would do anything for his brother's baby—had gone so far as to wed the woman who had tried to take Nicky away.

Once she'd thought he was the enemy. Yet everything she wanted for her sister's child, he'd tried to provide. Even a mother.

Nicky had been uppermost in her mind too when she accepted the arrangement. So why now did she have a hollow in her heart, an ache in her throat stemming from some undefined, deep-down hurt? Not a totally new sensation, but previously it had been associated with her sister. Now it was centred on Zandro.

Zandro was her husband, her lover. A considerate husband, an exciting lover.

No longer a threatening stranger, an adversary, he had become someone she looked forward to seeing every day. Someone she could depend on, trust, respect…love.

The knowledge burst on her like a flash of golden light. She loved Zandro. Deeply, irrevocably. Passionately.

He must have picked up something from her expression. 'What is it?' he asked her. 'Why are you looking at me like that?'

Tongue-tied, she shook her head. Zandro had been upfront with her about his motives for marrying her. But he'd specifically said he wasn't in love with her, although he wanted to sleep with her. If she told him of her shattering discovery would he accept it with pleasure, or be uncomfortable because he couldn't return her feelings?

Her love had become a burden to her sister, a shackle to be shaken off. That rejection from the person who was closest to her in all the world had pierced her deeply, made her wary of inviting another such wound to her heart. Zandro himself had warned her against making the same mistake with Nicky. And Zandro was the most self-sufficient person she had ever known, the least likely to need a smothering affection or appreciate an unwanted love. If he didn't—couldn't—reciprocate her newfound feelings she didn't think she could bear it.

She moistened her lips. 'I was thinking.'

'What about?' Then a strange, resigned expression stiffened his face. 'Nicky.'

'Yes,' she said quickly. It wasn't quite a lie. 'And the new baby.'

His brows drew together. She sensed a tension in him, some sharp displeasure. 'Perhaps when it arrives you won't be quite so obsessed with Nicky.'

Her fear of betraying herself making her super-sensitive, she became sharp. 'I'm not obsessed!'

For a moment she thought he regretted having used the word. But then his jaw set in a familiar fashion and his very silence reinforced the accusation.

'I've tried,' she said, 'to meet your…expectations—'

'Oh, sure,' he said witheringly. 'You've simply added pleasing me to everything you do for Nicky, haven't you? Wearing yourself out. Will my child be as important to you as your sister's?'

'Of course!' The question shocked her. 'It's my child too—ours. But…'

'I know.' He made an impatient gesture with one hand. 'Nicky is the most important thing in your life.'

But that, Cara realised, was no longer true. Of course she would never stop caring for Nicky, loving him, protecting him, but that was a different kind of love entirely—and right now Zandro filled her mind, her heart.

Perhaps he was right. She *had* been obsessed with making up to Nicky—*through* him—for having failed her sister.

Now she had something else to feel guilty about. She hadn't been giving enough attention to her husband, her marriage. If she had, this recognition of her love for him might have come sooner. And she might have won his love in return.

She'd assumed that sex was enough for him—plus the fact that their marriage gave Nicky a substitute mother. In her mind she'd made him a lesser man than he really was.

He'd asked for her companionship, her support, told her he wanted a real wife. Someone who wasn't wholly preoccupied by the child they shared, with sex on the side as an optional extra when Nicky was sleeping. He hadn't asked for her love…but in time perhaps he would want that, too.

Quietly she said, 'Our marriage is very important to me, Zandro.' She lifted her arms, her face to him.

'What?' Zandro queried, his hand going to her hair, his gaze questioning. 'What do you want, Cara?'

More than he'd offered when he asked her to marry him. More, perhaps, than he could give. She wanted…admitting it to herself, she heard the words in her mind…his love.

I want you to love me. Aloud, she whispered, 'I want you to take me to bed.'

At first he didn't move, and for a second or so she thought he was going to refuse her. Then he made an odd muffled sound in his throat, bent his head and kissed her with determined gentleness and restraint; and she kissed him back with passion, wanting to break through the barrier of his consideration, meet him on some primitive level where without words she could convey her love, force him to abandon the tight rein he kept on his emotions, and surrender to the moment.

When he tried to hold back she took the initiative and left him in no doubt of what she wanted.

'Cara,' he said, his voice grating, 'are you sure?'

'Yes!' She silenced him with her mouth, her hands raking into his hair, holding him to her, willing him to love her in every way possible.

At last he relented, gave her all she demanded of him—passion and tenderness and an intensity of sensation such as she'd never known. He gave her freely of his body, and took all that she offered in return. But afterwards, as they lay quietly, still entwined together, she didn't know if he'd understood what she'd tried to tell him without using words. Or if he'd really want to know.

She lay beside him, drinking in the sight of him, suddenly aware that he meant more to her than she had ever thought another person could. Even more than her twin, whose memory was already less constant now that Cara's days were filled with new and challenging relationships.

The two shall be one flesh. She and Lia had been one, before they were split apart in their mother's womb and became two separate people. Now Zandro was her 'other half.' A cliché. But like all clichés the phrase had endured because it had universal meaning.

The words hovered on her tongue, but her feelings were too new, too fragile, to speak aloud. While they remained unspoken she could hope. If she asked him point-blank if he loved her and Zandro turned the question aside the disappointment would be crushing. And if he lied, out of kindness and pity, perhaps even compunction at having married her without love, how would she know?

She laid her head against his shoulder, where he couldn't see the longing in her face, couldn't guess at her thoughts, and where she could hear the steady beating of his heart.

She was on the beach alone some days later, walking on the wet sand at the water's edge, when the first unmistakable stirring of the child in her womb brought her hands instinctively over her newly rounded belly. She stilled, every nerve attuned to this new sensation, and whispered foolishly, 'Hello, there.'

As if in response there was a fluttering against her fingers, and she lifted her face and laughed aloud at the blue sky overhead, thinking, 'I must tell Zandro.' She looked down at where her hands rested and said, 'I must tell your father.'

A rogue wave washed into the shore and foamed about her ankles, the spray almost reaching her knees. She felt an odd sensation just above her right ankle, a sudden numbness, and then the wave retreated, sucked back into the ocean, and the sensation became a piercing pain. Something had stung her. She looked at the glistening sand but it was empty except for soapy bubbles drifting across it.

By the time she got back to the house the pain was fierce and throbbing, and when she found Mrs Walker the housekeeper took one look at her white face and made her sit down while she explained what had happened.

Mrs Walker applied an ice pack to the swelling red flesh of her ankle and called Mrs Brunellesci. Domenico joined them and insisted she go to the nearest hospital.

When they got her there she was vomiting and dizzy, and then stomach cramps began and tears of pain and fear were running down her cheeks.

At some stage in the blur of white coats, strange faces and urgent questions Zandro appeared, his face gaunt and set in rigid lines. His eyes glittered with a strange angry light and his mouth looked grim. A voice in the background was saying something about '…an extreme reaction…quite rare…she couldn't tell us what it was…of course her pregnancy…danger of losing…'

A terrible fear filled her, and then someone swabbed her arm, there was a pinprick there, and the pain and the world receded.

She woke in a silent, dim room to find Zandro holding her hand. It was night, she realised. She felt spent, floaty, but there was no pain.

Zandro leaned forwards. 'Cara?'

Tiredly, trying to force away a heavy lump of dread that had settled in her chest, she closed her eyes again. But he said her name once more, urgently.

Without opening her eyes, she said, 'Did I lose your baby? I'm sorry…'

His hold on her hand tightened. 'The baby's all right. Not that it matters to me.' His voice sounded oddly unsteady.

She had to look at him then, staring in disbelief. 'What do you mean? I thought you wanted a child of your own.'

'I *have* a child…Nicky. And I hoped having a baby together would strengthen our marriage, bind you to me. But none of that is as important as your life. Losing the baby would be tragic, but it's you I couldn't bear to lose. I don't know how I'd live without you, *cara*.'

Maybe she was dreaming this, under the influence of the analgesia she'd been given. But it was a nice dream. She smiled drowsily. 'I love you,' she murmured. In a dream, she could say what was in her heart. Her eyelids drifted down again.

'What?' His grip on her hand momentarily became painful, making her eyes fly wide, and convincing her that she was truly awake after all, with Zandro's face only inches from hers, the familiar, aphrodisiac scent of him in her nostrils, his gaze pinioning her to the pillow behind her, fierce—incredulous.

'It's all right,' she said, 'if you can't love me back…' But then…if this wasn't a dream, he really had said those things…

She blinked, trying to force her fogged brain to function.

'What the hell do you mean,' Zandro demanded roughly, 'if I can't love you back? I think I fell fathoms deep in love the first time I set eyes on you!'

Cara blinked again, saying faintly, 'What?'

'Something happened—' his eyes burned into hers '—right there and then. My world shifted and I *knew* you. In a way I'd never known your sister. It hit me right between the eyes.'

Now she was definitely awake, listening with all her being, afraid to breathe, hypnotised by the fiery intensity in his eyes, the throbbing harshness in his voice.

'I told myself it was an aberration.' Remembered anger and self-disgust coloured his tone. 'Some weird phenomenon that would go away. But it got stronger all the time. It drove me crazy—I kept making excuses to touch you—kissing you when I couldn't fight it any longer, hating my own weakness. Making up stupid excuses, rationalisations that I knew damn well were nonsense. And when I found out who you really were…'

'You were furious,' she whispered. Not that she blamed him. It had been a monstrous deception to pull on anyone.

'Yes, but it explained a lot. I was angry that you'd felt the need to lie to me, and furious that I'd been taken in. My pride took a beating—I realised you hated me, believed I was some kind of callous brute. But when the idea of marrying you came to me…I knew it was right.'

'I didn't hate you, not once I'd seen you with Nicky. You said…our marriage was a logical solution.'

'Yes,' he said. 'But also…I felt here—' he thumped

a fist over his heart in the first purely Italian gesture she'd ever seen him use '—that it was meant to be. We belonged together. Though in my mind I knew it was too much to expect you'd feel the same. So I had to present the idea to you as a way to fulfil your obligation to your sister. Because I knew that was all that mattered to you. It still is.'

She heard the bitter note in his voice. 'No.' That was no longer true. Of course she would never stop caring for Nicky, loving him, protecting him, but right now Zandro filled her mind, her heart.

She tried to explain, making an effort to talk coherently. 'I hadn't been there for Lia when Rico was killed, and she was left with Nicky. When you told me how she'd been living I felt so guilty. Because somehow I knew. From when she said she was pregnant I'd had this horrible feeling of dread gnawing at me. If I'd followed my instincts and flown over she might not have become so desperate…might not have died.'

Tears stung, and Zandro put a hand over hers. 'She made her own decisions, Cara. Not good ones, but you tried your damnedest to put things right.'

'Yes.' Even after her charade was exposed, after marrying Zandro, she'd remained convinced that only giving all her devotion, all her time to Lia's child could make up for failing her sister.

Until Zandro had made her love him—and given her his love, though she'd been too blindly wrapped up in her self-imposed reparation to recognise it.

Zandro lifted a hand to her face and wiped the tears as they began to fall. 'I've upset you, *cara*. Maybe this is the wrong time—'

'No,' she choked. 'No. I was afraid you wouldn't

want…what I had to give. And maybe too…maybe I felt I didn't have a right to be happy.'

He scowled. 'For God's sake, why?'

'My sister lost everything—Rico, her baby…her life. As you said, I hadn't been able to save her. And then…I hadn't even kept my last promise to her. It wasn't fair that I gained so much by her death.'

'No one could have saved her, Cara! Death is never fair. And you did more for Nicky than she had any right to ask of you.' He held her face between his hands so she had to look into his eyes. 'If she really loved him she'd want Nicky to be happy above all else, wouldn't she? And you—surely she loved you and wanted your happiness too?'

She struggled with the concept, briefly, afraid to accept that after all the answer could be so simple. Afraid of grasping at a straw because she wanted so much for him to be right.

But he *was* right—it was so obvious when he pointed it out to her. Her own brush with death, and the knowledge that Zandro loved her, had finally cleared her mind of its confused sense of guilt, freed her from her self-imposed penance. 'Yes.' Cara at last relaxed, let her head fall against his shoulder, let his love flow over her, allowed hers to break free at last, and lifted her mouth to his kiss, accepting his passion and his need, that equalled hers.

EPILOGUE

NICKY was almost two when his little brother entered the world one stormy night. Zandro was by Cara's side, holding her hand as the midwife showed them their new son. Afterwards he brought Nicky to see them both, sitting him on the bed where Cara could put an arm about him and introduced him to the latest member of their family, asleep against her breast.

'Baby!' Nicky crowed, his eyes widening.

'Your baby brother,' she said. 'Liam.' Her eyes met Zandro's, silently expressing her gratitude that he'd agreed on the name.

'B'other,' Nicky said importantly. He'd been coached to expect one, but Cara hadn't been sure how much he'd understood.

Liam opened his eyes and Nicky giggled. 'Eyes!' he pointed out, delighted.

Zandro laughed. Cara unwrapped the baby and showed Nicky the baby had fingers, too, and toes. When the toddler got bored, Zandro took him off to his grandmother for a while, and came back as Cara was tucking Liam into the bassinet at the side of the bed.

'Nicky's telling Mamma all about his new brother. And how are you?' He himself on the side of the bed and, taking her hand, searched her face.

'I'm fine.'

He looked down at their linked hands. 'If I'd known what it would be like,' he said, 'I never would have

185

allowed you to go through that.' He looked up with anguish in his eyes, and something else that made her breath stop in her throat. 'Have you any idea,' he asked huskily, his voice shaking in a way she'd never heard before, his hands tightening on hers so much his grip was painful, 'how much I love you? I didn't realise myself until you brought our baby into the world and I held you both in my arms.'

For moments she wasn't able to speak, her eyes blurring with tears. 'I love you too. You're all I ever wanted in a man, Zandro. More than I deserve.' And he'd given her the two most wonderful gifts in the world. His child, and his love.

'That's not true. I'm the luckiest man in the world.' Reaching for her, he pulled her into his arms, but gently. He kissed her mouth with fervour, savouring the way she returned the kiss.

Liam squawked, wriggling inside his wrapping the bassinet. Reluctantly his parents parted, and looked down at their newborn son, whose eyes were open, apparently inspecting them with interest.

'You've been fed,' Cara told him. 'Now you're supposed to sleep.'

The baby's mouth turned down, and a frown wrinkled his forehead, making his parents laugh.

Zandro said, 'He promises to be as much of a handful as his brother.' He took one of the tiny hands that had escaped its wrapping, and watched the baby instantly clasp one of his fingers.

'Your son,' she said.

'My second son.'

She smiled at him. 'Nicky's as much ours as Liam, isn't he?'

'Yes,' Zandro said. 'As we are each other's. A family. Mum, Dad and the kids. But no more children. I'm not having you—'

She raised a hand and put it over his mouth. 'Shh. It's not just your decision, Zandro. Besides, it's worth it. One day I might like a daughter, and I have a feeling you would, too.'

He took her hand away to kiss the palm, his mouth lingering. 'You'd go through that again?' He shook his head. 'I never knew I could love another human being this way. Thank you, Cara. Of course you will do as you wish.'

'Always?' She gave him a mischievous smile.

Suspiciously he said, 'Perhaps not always. I won't have you endanger yourself. It's my right as your husband to prevent that.'

Wisely, Cara didn't argue. Not now. There would be times when they'd argue, and times when she'd give in, but Zandro already knew he couldn't always win. And their love would keep them from tearing each other apart, or either of them imposing their will on the other.

They had a marriage, a family and each other, united in unbreakable bonds of love. It was enough.

More than that. It was the whole wonderful world.

MILLS & BOON®

Live the emotion

His Boardroom Mistress

In February 2005 By Request brings
back three favourite novels by our
bestselling Mills & Boon authors:

The Husband Assignment
by Helen Bianchin
The Baby Verdict *by Cathy Williams*
The Bedroom Business *by Sandra Marton*

Seduction from 9-5...
and after hours!

On sale 4th February 2005

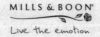

MILLS & BOON

Volume 8
on sale from
6th February
2005

Lynne
GRAHAM

International Playboys

The Unfaithful Wife

4 FREE

BOOKS AND A SURPRISE GIFT!

We would like to take this opportunity to thank you for reading this Mills & Boon® book by offering you the chance to take FOUR more specially selected titles from the Modern Romance™ series absolutely FREE! We're also making this offer to introduce you to the benefits of the Reader Service™—

- ★ **FREE home delivery**
- ★ **FREE gifts and competitions**
- ★ **FREE monthly Newsletter**
- ★ **Exclusive Reader Service offers**
- ★ **Books available before they're in the shops**

Accepting these FREE books and gift places you under no obligation to buy, you may cancel at any time, even after receiving your free shipment. Simply complete your details below and return the entire page to the address below. You don't even need a stamp!

YES! Please send me 4 free Modern Romance books and a surprise gift. I understand that unless you hear from me, I will receive 6 superb new titles every month for just £2.69 each, postage and packing free. I am under no obligation to purchase any books and may cancel my subscription at any time. The free books and gift will be mine to keep in any case.

P5ZED

Ms/Mrs/Miss/Mr ....Initials ....
BLOCK CAPITALS PLEASE

Surname ....

Address ....

....

....Postcode.............................

Send this whole page to:
UK: FREEPOST CN81, Croydon, CR9 3WZ

Offer valid in UK only and is not available to current Reader service subscribers to this series. Overseas and Eire please write for details. We reserve the right to refuse an application and applicants must be aged 18 years or over. Only one application per household. Terms and prices subject to change without notice. Offer expires 29th April 2005. As a result of this application, you may receive offers from Harlequin Mills & Boon and other carefully selected companies. If you would prefer not to share in this opportunity please write to The Data Manager, PO Box 676, Richmond, TW9 1WU.

Mills & Boon® is a registered trademark owned by Harlequin Mills & Boon Limited.
Modern Romance™ is being used as a trademark. The Reader Service™ is being used as a trademark.